the christmas carols

kali hart   **kate tilney**   **lana dash**

ivy and the ghost of christmas past

Kali Hart

one

. . .

IVY

As the plane touches down on the Anchorage, Alaska runway, two thoughts are on repeat in my head. One: my sisters are going to kill me. Two: this is the most insane thing I've ever done in my life.

I resist the urge to grip either of the occupied armrests as my seat rumbles and shakes. I *hate* sitting in the middle seat. It's why I buy my tickets months in advance. To avoid being wedged between the tallest man alive, whose elbow has apologetically been in my side most of this flight, and the lady who's been sleeping like the dead since the second we hit altitude. Tall man and I shared more than one *oh my god* look as her snores cycled between throaty rumbles and head back, mouth open gasps.

But that's what a last-minute ticket during the holidays gets you.

I close my eyes and try to force my breathing to slow down. It's an epic fail.

Fucking Betty White.

Okay, let's be real. I *love* Betty White. Especially the Grandma Annie version from my all-time favorite movie. But I didn't expect her to be in my dreams last night. Or to encourage me to do something completely irrational. How the hell do I explain this to my sisters? We're triplets for crying out loud. We're supposed to be more in sync than this. Supposed to know when one of us is about to go off the rails.

Besides, I'm the calculated one. I have a carefully laid out plan for every occasion. So many plans in fact, that it drives my sisters bonkers.

Yet, after a dream involving *Grandma Annie* dancing and chanting around my bed in her ceremony garments, I started throwing things in my overnight bag with sleep still in my eyes. The dream, the mildly inappropriate comments about a man from my past, had my heart racing in a way nothing had in...well, way too long. Grandma Annie insisted I should be spending Christmas with *him*, and something inside me knew she was right. I bought the last plane ticket for the next flight out.

I'm so far off the freaking rails it's not even funny.

My sisters—Holly and Merry—don't even know I've left Denver, much less the contiguous United States.

I haven't been able to sleep a wink on this trip, unlike my aisle seat neighbor, who's *still* sawing logs even as the plane rolls toward the terminal. I'm too spun up about the call I have to make to my sisters. How do I tell them I probably won't be home for Christmas—the first Christmas without our mom? And, even if I manage to smooth that out, what am I going to say to Luke after all this time?

An automatic flutter of butterfly wings erupts in my belly at the mere thought of him. I can almost see Grandma

4

Annie smiling down on me like some guardian angel, pleased with my bravery. Ah. She's proud of me.

Then the panic sets in.

What the hell was I thinking?

This is a *terrible* idea.

When Luke and I last saw each another, emotions of all varieties were high.

Three years ago, the summer before I started law school, I landed an internship with a family law firm in Caribou Creek. Only a month outside of a toxic breakup, it had sounded like a dream come true. A cute, rugged town tucked in the mountains. A practice focused on helping families in need. There weren't any cons in this scenario. Only a spreadsheet full of pros.

But I didn't expect anything on my spreadsheet to look like Luke.

As the plane nears the terminal, I reluctantly fish my phone out of my purse. If I didn't fear that my sisters would send out a massive search party for me, I'd leave my phone off for another day or two. But I'm not known for going off-grid. I'm the one who has a meticulous schedule with a desk drawer full of planners to prove how serious I am about those time blocks. Since we're supposed to be baking Christmas cookies in my kitchen tonight, I have no choice but to rip off the Band-aid before I lose cell service.

I stare at the phone resting in unfamiliar, shaky hands. They don't even look like my hands. Do I remember the pin to unlock my phone? I feel like I've stepped through a looking glass. I'm not sure what's up or down anymore.

Maybe this was a mistake.

I never told my sisters about Luke. I never knew how to explain him, or what might've been sparking between us but never had a chance to become anything. My heart was still battered and bruised. Steal walls were fortified around its remains. I didn't trust myself when it came to picking men. So my instant connection with Luke was too suspect for my comfort. I never allowed anything to transpire beyond a crush.

Luke, though patient, was not shy about his interest in me.

I thought the memories would've faded by now. I wouldn't still think about him. Or wonder what could've been if I'd just been ready to take a chance. But I was determined to stay the course, finish law school and get my degree. I wasn't going to let anything stop me. Not the trauma from my useless ex. And certainly not a *something* over a perfect guy that couldn't even be put into words.

I just didn't expect the pining I'd *still* feel for Luke over three years later. The dull ache in my chest that never quite goes away.

A sharp elbow in my side, accompanied by a genuine apology from my window seat neighbor, knocks the phone out of my hands. It tumbles into my purse amid the clicking echo of seat belts unbuckling throughout the cabin.

"First time to Alaska?" The woman who's been snoring the whole flight asks as though we've been friends for the past three and a half hours.

"Second." I dig in my purse for my phone, but it's the Christmas card I find first. One June Ashburn sent me. It's probably the real reason for the Betty White dream. I helped June and her husband draft a will during my internship. She's sent me a Christmas card every year since. But this is the first time she's mentioned Luke.

The words *I think Luke misses you* pop out at me as if they're written in bold red ink.

"You going to Caribou Creek?" she asks, nodding at the

card's image of the charming town as the front of the cabin starts to deplane.

"Yeah."

"Careful you don't get snowed in. Unless that's what you want."

"I checked the weather—"

"That's cute and all, but those little mountain towns have their own weather patterns. Just be careful, huh?"

When I visited Caribou Creek the first time, it was during the summer. But I'm from Denver. I'm not exactly a stranger to mountain-based weather. Or snowstorms. As long as I can find a Wi-Fi signal on Christmas Eve so I can Skype in for the holiday I'll likely be missing at home, I can work around the rest.

A good attorney can adapt to any situation.

The mere thought is enough to twist my stomach in knots as I follow the last of the passengers off the plane. My bar exam results will be in any day. Though I'm confident I passed, the sliver of doubt is enough to keep me from getting cocky. My entire future depends on those results. Just passing isn't enough for me. I want the highest possible score to help lock in my dream job of working for the largest family law firm in Denver.

I've barely stepped into the terminal when Ariana Grande belts out a Christmas song from inside my purse. Dammit. One of my sisters is calling *me*. Holly. The one who will take this news the hardest.

I step off to the side, take a deep breath, and prepare to break both my sisters' hearts.

two

. . .

IVY

The drive to Caribou Creek is snowy, treacherous, and one I should *not* have attempted in a compact rental car. My knuckles are still white and aching from how tightly I clenched the steering wheel the entire two hundred miles north.

"Checking in?" The woman behind the lodge counter smiles at me sweetly. It's the first bit of reassurance I've felt since that crazy dream and impulsive plane ticket purchase. Spoiler alert: my sisters did *not* take my surprise news well. Holly laid on the guilt pretty heavily about missing our first Christmas together without Mom. Especially since I gave some lame excuse about visiting my old boss for the holidays.

"Yes!"

"Name?"

"Ivy Carol."

Her fingers click quickly across the keys, but before I can

tell her I don't have a reservation courtesy of my impulsive decision to hop on the first available flight this morning, I hear a familiar voice from my past.

"Ivy Carol? Is that really you?"

I turn and lock eyes with the sweetest elderly man in existence, Art Matthews. Caribou Creek's sole family law representation. The last time I was in town, we celebrated his eightieth birthday. The only reason I know he's still practicing is because I looked up the firm online. Thanks to my encouragement, Art took my advice about getting a website. I scoured it a hundred times while I waited in the terminal, searching for any hint of his nephew, Luke. But there wasn't a single photo on the firm's site that captured the man I haven't been able to stop pining over these past three years.

"Mr. Matthews!" I wrap him in a warm hug, so damn happy to see a familiar face.

"It's Art," he corrects. "Or have you forgotten that?"

As I pull away, I can't help the automatic search I do for Luke. "I haven't forgotten."

"Didn't know you were coming back to town."

"It was a last minute decision—"

"Ms. Carol, I don't have a reservation under your name," the woman behind the counter kindly interrupts.

"I didn't make one."

Her smile drops. "You didn't?"

"Is the crazy expensive suite the only room available?" I tease, earning a chuckle from Art. The sound of the old man's laughter takes me back to the best month of my life. I can't believe how much I've missed Luke stopping by the firm every morning to drop off coffee. It was the little things I'm starting to realize that were the big things. I just hope he's happy to see me when I finally track him down.

"There aren't any rooms available."

My smile is the next one to die. "Really?"

"I'm sorry. Christmas is a very popular time in Caribou Creek."

My stomach twists in knots at the unexpected dilemma. I felt certain few soul would venture to a middle-of-Alaska mountain town in winter. It's a charming place, but not exactly a destination trip when it's ten below zero on a warm day. "You don't have anything?" The words crack as they leave my lips. I will *not* cry.

"Afraid not."

"You can stay at Luke's cabin," Art offers, his kind smile loosening the worst of the knots churning in my stomach. I wasn't planning to run into Luke until at least tomorrow when I'd slept off the jet lag and formed a plan. I have no clue what I'm going to say to him, and I need time to figure it out. "He's out on a guided hunt."

"He's not here?" Relief and disappointment go to war inside my chest. Did I really fly all the way to Alaska only to miss the man I came to hunt down?

"He took out a group day before yesterday. Not expected back until Christmas Eve." Christmas Eve. That's three days from now. It's the day Holly wants me to fly home, but I guess a Skype call is the best I can promise. And three days gives me plenty of time to figure out what to tell Luke.

"You don't think he'll mind?"

"Not at all."

Luke's interest in me wasn't secret when I was here last time. Art was constantly dropping hints that we'd be good together. I think the old man felt genuinely disappointed when I left. Maybe he's still trying to match make. The last thing I want to do is break his heart when I leave again —

because I can't stay—but I don't have another alternative. I'm not about to drive back to Anchorage in the dark or sleep in my car in these frigid temperatures.

"I can put you on the list in case there's a cancellation," the woman behind the counter offers.

"Yes, please." With any luck, I'll be back at the hotel before Luke returns home. Just me being in town will be enough of a surprise. Especially since I have no idea if he's moved on. Maybe he has a girlfriend. The thought sours in my stomach.

It's a risk I'll have to take since Betty White was pretty tight lipped on the obstacles I might have to face.

three

. . .

LUKE

I can't decide if I'm pleased or irritated that the entire group I took caribou hunting hit their limit two days earlier than anticipated. I *should* be happy to be home early, but I fucking hate the holidays. The only reason I stick it out year to year is to make sure Uncle Art doesn't have to spend it alone. My sister is flighty and rarely in the state over the holidays, so I've accepted the obligation.

I lose the battle with a massive yawn as I pull into my driveway. I love the open wilderness, but I always come home with a greater appreciation for my bed. After a hot shower, that special order king-size mattress is my only destination. With any luck, I'll sleep right through the town festival tomorrow.

As I cut the engine, twinkling lights catch my eyes. I squint at the corner window, certain I'm hallucinating. Because it looks like there's a fucking Christmas tree in *my* living room window. Any hope that sleep deprivation is going to explain this shit away dies when the lights change from solid white to a variety of colors.

"The fuck..."

The only person I can think of who would be brave enough to invite themselves into my house and decorate for the holidays is my sister, Maggie. It's her decorations I've been storing in my crawlspace since she took off on her second year-long trip to see the world.

The second I open the front door, my ear drums are assaulted by some female musician with an usually high voice belting out a Christmas tune about Santa.

I kick off my boots and shrug out of my snow-dusted coat, reining in my annoyance. If my sister's back from her adventure already, something's wrong. She doesn't need the asshole version of me to make things worse. Even if she *did* make the holidays vomit all over my house. Maggie understands my disdain for the season. She went through that horrible Christmas Eve with me, but her resilience kept her love of the holidays alive. Mine, on the other hand, died a quick and painful death that awful night.

I need a beer if I'm going to put a hint of a smile on for Maggie. Fuck, is that garland hanging from the island in my kitchen? The fridge jingles when I open it, courtesy of sleigh bells wrapped around the handle.

I can't twist the cap off a bottle of Caribou Creek Stout fast enough. I lift it to my lips, turn, and nearly choke.

It's not Maggie dancing around the Christmas tree.

It's a ghost from my past.

Ivy Carol.

I haven't slept in thirty-six hours. Sleep deprivation is obviously doing a number on me. Did I go to the wrong fucking house and someone hasn't noticed? She hasn't turned around. Maybe I'm seeing things and when I realize who the woman really is, we'll both be horrified. But I can't stop staring at the hips in leggings adorned in Christmas lights swaying enthusiastically to the beat of the music.

When she turns around, my heart stops.

Ivy's eyes go wide, as if she's been caught robbing a bank vault. The round green ornament dangling from her fingers falls to the floor and bounces off a fluffy skirt that looks like an abdominal snowman pelt beneath the tree.

Setting the bottle on the counter, I march into the living room, desperate to capture whatever seconds I can before the sleep-deprived fantasy fades into smoke. Three and a half years is a long fucking time to be stuck on someone. To still dream about them almost nightly. To wonder what would be different if I'd just taken a chance and kissed her before she drove away… Would she have stayed?

Without a beat of hesitation, I sweep her into my arms, grip her cheek, and capture the lips I've waited forever to taste. I do it all without uttering a single word. Without warning. And Ivy melts into me half a second after my lips meet hers, wrapping her arms around my neck and surrendering to my hungry mouth.

If anyone is brave enough to wake me from this dream, it'll be the last fucking thing they ever do.

four

. . .

IVY

When Luke breaks apart the kiss, my legs are no better than overcooked noodles. If he wasn't holding on to my waist so tightly, I'd be a puddle on the floor for sure. I've fantasized about this first kiss, but the reality has completely caught me by surprise. My entire body buzzes from the sheer force of it. The possessiveness. I've never experienced anything like it before. I could blame the unexpectedness of the kiss, but a voice that sounds suspiciously like Betty White in my head calls bullshit.

I shiver.

Luke's dark eyes drench with desire. I know I'm right because I've seen it once before in a heated moment when I almost gave in three years ago. *Almost.*

I've lost all ability for rational thinking.

The only thoughts swirling in my mind now are dirty. Dirty enough to get me on Santa's naughty list *very* quickly.

Words still unspoken, I can't help but wonder if he's

going to whisk me off to the bedroom and have his way with me. Right here. Right now. I'd ask him, if I was capable of using words. But I'm panting too damn hard and still struck dumb from shock. I wonder what he'd think if he knew I slept in his bed last night. In his t-shirt. And what the hell is going through his mind right now? Did his uncle tip him off about me?

"You're here."

"Yes."

"You're *really* here."

"In the flesh."

I lean in, hoping for another taste of those delicious lips. But Luke steps back, dropping his arms. I stumble from the unsteady legs but manage to stay upright with concentrated effort. "*Why* are you here?" His gaze lifts from mine and stares hard at the Christmas tree I've nearly finished decorating. The ice is his tone is chilling enough to rival the Alaskan wilderness right now.

"Do you like it?"

"No."

His answer delivers a punch I wasn't expecting, and my weak but hopeful smile drops completely. "It's your tree—"

"It's not." His harsh tone cuts like a razor. "Take it down."

"What?"

"You heard me." He turns and struts down the hall. The bedroom door slams behind him leaving me even more confused than ever.

I expected some resistance from Luke when he discovered I was here. I'm the one who turned him down that summer. Even though deep down I *wanted* to say yes. But I suspected my heart couldn't survive surrendering to him and then leaving. I was fighting the fall. A fall that would've kept me from going to law school or taking the bar exam. Of following my dream to practice family law and make a real difference in people's lives.

So why are you here then?

The voice in my head sounds an awful lot like Grandma Annie. Automatically, I scan the room. Though unless Betty White has come back from the dead, I know she isn't standing in a corner nearby. Is it too late to blame the jet lag on this insanity?

"You tell me," I mutter in answer.

The Christmas lights on the tree switch from solid white to multi-color, causing me to turn around. I'm half a dozen ornaments from being finished decorating it. I'm *not* taking it down just because Luke is being extra grumpy. The man is probably tired and not thinking straight. Add in the surprise of finding me in his house… He used to tell me about the guided trips he led and how little sleep he'd get while on them. "He just needs some rest."

Where are you sleeping, Ivy?

Okay, Betty White. Get out of my head please. This is getting creepy.

My gaze drifts down the hall to the closed bedroom door. It's the only bed in the cabin. And the couch … has seen better days.

You didn't come all this way to sleep on that old thing.

I gasp, as if Grandma Annie herself had just handed over the baby maker quilt and winked at me. I wait for any more inappropriate words of wisdom to come, but her voice has fallen silent inside my head.

I glance between the couch and the closed door.

Betty White is right. I *didn't* come all this way to sleep on a ratty couch. I didn't plan to immediately seduce the man, either. But hell. I didn't show up with any kind of plan, which means I'm running blind. Since Luke showed up two days earlier than expected, I'm winging it. A good attorney can wing it. *Right?*

I'm *sooo* off the fucking rails. I half expect my phone to vibrate. One of my sisters sensing that something is up. But the phone doesn't ring. I have to make a choice.

I tiptoe down the hall and press my ear to the door. The hiss of a shower leaves me hopeful that I can simply sneak into his room and crawl under the covers. Maybe he'll sleep like the dead and not even notice me. Or maybe we'll have wild, hot sex all night long. I squeeze my thighs together at the thought. God I could use a good orgasm I didn't give myself.

But will Luke be interested when he finds out I'm not staying this time either?

"Never again," I mutter about my lack of planning as I sneak into the room and change into the t-shirt I stole last night. The only light comes from the ajar bathroom door. A yawn assaults me as I crawl beneath the covers. If Luke doesn't want to share his bed, he's going to have to carry me out of it.

five

. . .

LUKE

The scent of peppermint drifts lazily to me, taking me back to a time when the world revolved around one woman. When I lived to see her smile every morning and refused to accept that she would leave. If sleep deprivation is the only way to be close to Ivy, then I'll keep myself tired forever.

A warm body shifts against mine in the dark room. My dick's already wide awake thanks to the memories conjured by that peppermint shampoo.

Peppermint shampoo.

My tired eyes snap wide open.

Ivy's curvy body is tucked up against mine, her back to my chest. Her ass softly wriggles against my throbbing cock. No wonder the fucker is standing at attention.

The brief memories of last night assault me. Discovering Christmas had thrown up all over my fucking house. Ivy dancing around the tree with an ornament dangling from her fingers. The earth-shattering kiss with a ghost who turned out not to be a ghost at all.

And now she's in my bed.

The memory of *how* is one I can't place. After a hot shower last night, the last thing I remember is collapsing in bed.

I dare to move the arm wrapped around her and drop my hand to her hip. My fingers dig into her soft, exposed skin, promising me she's real. Fuck me. She's wearing one of my t-shirts. How many nights has she been sleeping in my bed? If I'd known she was in Caribou Creek, I would've called the hunt early and refunded everyone's money just to have more time.

Ivy moans softly as my hand greedily caresses her thigh. She shimmies against me, turning slightly. Her thighs open a sliver, parting in what seems like an invitation. Making me wish time would stand still so I never had to leave this room.

Time.

I have no fucking clue why she's here or if she plans to stay. I might only have a day or two to convince her this is where she belongs. But why does it have to be at fucking Christmas time? I hate the holidays and the loss it reminds me of. The pain I relive year after year.

But remembering the sparkle in her eyes when she turned around at the Christmas tree and spotted me … I can't imagine a torture I wouldn't endure to see her happy. To see that glow every day.

My fingers graze the edge of her panties and she moans again. Her face turns and her hand searches for my cheek. "Luke?" she whispers, my name a fucking dream coming from those lips.

"Yes, sweetheart?"

"Touch me?"

My dick throbs at her plea. *Calm the fuck down.* "Are you sure this is what you want?"

"It's the only thing I want."

I slide one finger along the silk of her panties, pressing against the damp fabric to tease her swollen button. Fuck she's so wet I might lose my damn mind. Before she tries to leave me again, I'm going to claim that tight, perfect pussy for my own. But when I do, she'll be begging me to be inside her. Tonight—or this morning as I have no concept of how long I've been asleep—I'm going to bring her to heights of pleasure she'll never forget.

If she leaves again, I'll have ruined her for all other men.

Because Ivy Carol is mine.

I'll make her believe it one delicious touch at a time.

I stroke her pussy through the silk, pressing firmly against that button. She whimpers at my touch, parting her thighs wider. She rocks her hips to the rhythm of my touch. When she lets out a moan, I take my hand away.

"Is this my t-shirt?" I growl against her ear as that same hand slides up her soft skin beneath my shirt, discovering no bra and hard nipples. I take my time teasing each peak, gently pinching them between my thumb and index finger, enjoying every sexy noise that escape her throat.

"Y—yes. It's your—*shirt!*" The last word comes out an octave higher.

"Good to know your nipples are so sensitive, sweetheart. I bet they'd like my mouth on them." I slowly push up the shirt, exposing her bountiful tits to me in the dim light. Fuck me they're perfect. I take the closest nipple in my mouth, lazily stroking my tongue around it. I cup her other tit in my hand, gently squeezing it. One of these days,

I'll rub my dick between these beauties and cum all over them.

Because I can't leave out her other nipple, I straddle her body to give me better access.

"Luke," she moans.

"Yes, baby?"

"I want you."

I let out a deep, low chuckle. "Soon, baby. But not yet."

After I've given both nipples ample and equal attention with my mouth, I slide down her body, kissing a trail past her belly button. When I reach the top of her panties, I grip the hem with my teeth and tug them down. Inhaling her sweet scent nearly does me in. It takes all my restraint not to plow into her now and claim her as my own.

Patience.

With her panties pulled partway down, I dip my tongue into her folds. She moans my name and lifts her hips. I tease her nub with lazy circles until she arches hard into my face. When I pull back, she audibly groans.

"You're going to kill me," she says.

"No." I peel away her panties, tossing them across the room for me to find and keep later. "I'm going to take you to a place you've never been, baby." I scoop my hands beneath her ass and lift her fully exposed pussy to my eager mouth. As much as I want to devour her like she's a starving man's last meal, I force myself to slow down. To savor every lick.

When I slip my tongue into her channel, she bucks.

I place my hand over her stomach and press her back down into the mattress. "I've got you, baby. Don't you worry."

I feel her body relax and she opens wider.

With agonizing leisure, I use every stroke and flicker of

my tongue to take her over the edge. When she fists her hand in my hair, shoving my face tight against her pussy, I decide I can live without oxygen. I just can't live without *her*.

Ivy comes hard and loud, her pussy convulsing around my tongue. My cock throbs. The fucker's angry he's not the one inside her tight channel right now. I damn near nut as I drink in every last drop of her ecstasy.

Only when her body stills do I break my lips apart from hers. I lock eyes with Ivy as I run my tongue along my lips, lapping up every last drop. "You taste divine, baby. I could eat you out all day. Stay through New Year's and we never even have to leave this bed."

six

· · ·

IVY

Freshly showered, I search for my panties on still wobbly legs. Never in my life have I had an orgasm that powerful. I'd only ever read about them in romance novels. I didn't think they were real. Why the hell didn't I give in to Luke sooner?

A single chime of my phone pulls my attention to the screen and a text from my bestie wanting to know if the bar exam results have come back yet.

Oh right.

I resisted Luke because my life is back in Denver.

Which makes what happened between us all the more problematic. Where's Grandma Annie when I need her?

Honestly, I haven't thought about the bar exam since Art dropped me off at Luke's remote cabin two days ago. And because the signal here is weak at best and I haven't been able to figure out the Wi-Fi password, I haven't even checked to see if results were posted. It seems less likely they'll be out before Christmas the closer the holiday gets.

After one last sweep of the bedroom, I give up on finding my favorite pair of panties. I glance at my suitcase. I *could* get dressed. Or I could stay wrapped in a towel that conveniently falls to the floor in Luke's kitchen. I'm hungry for breakfast. But I'm hungrier for him.

I tiptoe down the hall to surprise him, trying to come up with some cutesy quip about unwrapping a Christmas present early with each quiet step.

The aroma of bacon and eggs drifts to me as I find Luke standing at the stove, flipping an omelet. My heart melts a little. *He remembered.*

"Luke?"

"Hmm?"

"Merry Christmas." As he turns his head, I drop the towel like I planned. But before I can say the line I rehearsed in my head, I hear another voice.

"Tree looks good, Luke."

I drop to the ground like I'm taking fire and scramble for the towel. Son of a bitch. No one warned me Art was here! It's only the island that's keeping me shielded. For now. Luke has the audacity to grin from above at my dilemma. There's no way squatting naked like this is sexy. Not with all my curves. Damn that donut shop down the street from my apartment.

Luke crouches down slowly, like he has all the time in the world. He helps me wrap the towel around my body and lifts me to my feet. His hand drops possessively to my hip, tugging me against his side. If I wasn't wrapped in a towel, this might feel more special.

But I feel Art's curious eyes on me. I'm pretty sure if you

give an eighty-three-year-old man a heart attack at Christmas, it's a ticket straight to hell.

"I, uh, dropped a bobby pin." Never mind that my hair is still wet and hanging loosely over my shoulders. "I think it's gone."

Luke turns back toward the pan on the stove, flipping an omelet as if nothing happened.

"I stopped by to invite you both to the Christmas Festival," Art says, staring awkwardly at the counter. "I can never convince Luke to join me. But I thought you might enjoy it while you're here. Maybe you can change his mind."

"You won't," Luke chimes in, his attention fixated on the pan.

His instant dismissal reminds me of his reaction to finding a Christmas tree in his living room. One that he claims isn't his. Is it Christmas he hates or did I put up decorations that belong to an ex and hit a sore spot?

"That sounds lovely, Art. I'd love to join you. Why don't I go get dressed and you can tell me all about it?" I scurry down the hall and close the bedroom door behind me. I press my back to it and slide to the floor.

You didn't die of embarrassment, did you?

The voice is back.

"It was a close call," I grumble.

You just going to sit there or you going to get dressed?

Betty White's voice is stern but coated in a sweetness that makes it impossible to be mad at her. *If* she was actually real. Either way, it's enough to force me to my feet and start rifling through my suitcase for something appropriately cute for both men. I'm bummed Luke isn't interested in the Christmas Festival, but it would be rude to turn Art down when he came all this way. I've missed him.

Bet that job offer is still open.

"Bet it's not. Art has to be close to retirement." Great. Now I'm talking to the Grandma Annie voice. If Luke or Art catch me talking to myself, I'm pretty sure they'll eagerly welcome my departure from Caribou Creek. Whenever that is. I'm not expected back at work until January. What if I stayed a few extra days?

The warring thoughts in my head make me really regret not making a plan. Because a plan has action steps and a predictable outcome. A known target. I have no idea what happens when I leave Caribou Creek. Is this simply a holiday rendezvous or could this be … more?

"You sure you won't come?" I hear Art ask Luke as I pad quietly down the hallway toward the kitchen.

"You know how I feel about the festival."

"I know, son. But do you think she'd want you living this way?"

I freeze at the word *she*. The way Art says this makes me think Luke lost someone special. Oh shit! Did he lose a wife during the holidays and I put out all her decorations to remind him of it? This is so not happening.

With breath halted in my lungs, I wait for Luke to say something. Anything.

"This isn't the way to honor your mother's memory, Luke." Art's words are gentle, like a hug. I feel its embrace as if he's speaking the words to me too. Guilt squeezes my chest. Would my mom be upset that I ran off to Alaska for the holidays and abandoned my sisters? Or would she applaud me for taking a chance on my heart for once?

"Ah, Ivy. You look lovely." Art's smile eases the ache I feel inside my chest for both me and for Luke. "We best be going. It's a full day you know."

I glance at Luke, silently pleading for him to change his

mind. But I know what I'm asking of him and can't voice the words. I touch his arm. "Will I still have a place to stay when I get back?" I mean to tease him. To lighten the mood.

"You'll always have a place here, Ivy. Always."

seven

. . .

LUKE

I blame Maggie's fucking Christmas tree for this mess. If it weren't for her holiday decorations littered all over my house, I wouldn't have felt so trapped within the logs. I'd have stayed home and caught up on some much-needed sleep.

But I didn't. I kept busy with mindless chores until there was nothing left to do. First, I thoroughly plowed my long, winding driveway and then shot a text to Uncle Art. Ivy's little rental car could easily make the trek up it now.

Then I restocked wood for the fireplace and cleaned the kitchen from breakfast. A shower followed, one that was supposed to calm me down. Let me sleep. Fuck it all, I should be exhausted.

But here I am, in the middle of Caribou Creek during their annual Christmas festival. Abandoning my plans to take down all the holiday decorations before Ivy returns. The second I reached for the first ornament on the tree, the image of Ivy's curvy body moving to the beat of the music replayed in my mind.

Reminding me exactly how fucking bad I wanted to be inside her this morning.

Tonight, I'm making her mine. Ticking clock be damned.

Falling in love with Ivy more than three years ago was effortless. Something that happened the moment I saw her. I've never told this to another person, because they'd call me a fucking sap, but I swear my soul recognized hers. As if we'd already spent lifetimes together and were finding each other again.

Except she left to chase her dreams, and I couldn't allow myself to be the one to hold her back.

But this time, dammit, I want to be selfish. I want her to stay.

The main streets are blocked off from Rose's Diner to the Caribou Creek Brewery so people can wander around without worrying about traffic. Vendors brave enough to deal with the seven-degree temperature are stationed along the sidewalks, propane heaters keeping them thawed out. Sort of. Muffled conversation lifts from the growing crowd, taking me back to a simpler time.

I haven't attended a single Christmas festival since Mom died. It feels like there's an ice pick in my heart right now.

But that sharp pain fades the moment I spot Ivy handing a cup of hot chocolate to Art. Her smile is illuminating. One I'll never forget as long as I live. Even if she leaves again. She's the only one for me.

I weave my way through the crowd, turning several heads. Damn small town. Most of these people know how much I avoid anything to do with Christmas aside from a quiet family dinner with Art. Their shocked expressions say it all. I nod a few hellos and keeping moving through the masses to find Ivy.

"Luke Matthews, is that really you?" June Ashburn stops me with a gentle hand on my bicep. I track Ivy with my gaze, noting her and Uncle Art stop at a vendor selling baked goods. It gives me a moment to answer June.

"How are you, Mrs. Ashburn?"

"Fabulous! Did you hear I'm going to be a grandma again?"

"Congratulations. Who this time?" As much as I'm eager to get to Ivy, I can clearly hear my mother's voice in my head telling me to take my time. She always loved talking to people at this festival. Always gave them the kind of attention that never made them feel rushed or unimportant. It's the same way Ivy always was with Art, in or outside the office.

"Zach and Riley. Baby number two!" June gives me the once over, her gaze sweeping up and down. "When are you going to start working on a family? I know you want one."

I regret allowing June to con this information out of me one night at the brewery. It was weeks after Ivy left. What I wanted had never been clearer. But the key component to that dream—Ivy Carol—was gone. I pat June on the shoulder. "I'm working on it."

"Heard your girl is back in town." The twinkle in her eyes is suspect, but before I can call her out on it, her husband waves at her from across the street. "Good luck, Luke. I mean that. And Merry Christmas."

"Merry Christmas." Surprisingly, the words don't taste so sour leaving my lips. Mom's been gone five years now. The sting *has* lessened. And Art is right, as much as I hate to admit it. She wouldn't want me hiding from the celebration.

She'd have been disappointed. Maybe I just needed someone to remind me.

I spot Ivy and Art moving to another vendor booth and weave through the crowd, refusing to be stopped until I reach my woman. I know she plans to leave again, but I'm going to do everything in my power to convince her to stay.

Stepping up behind her at a scarf vendor, I drop my hands to her hips and my lips to her ear. "I'd like to see you in that red one." I kiss the top of her ear. "And nothing else."

She glances back, over her shoulder, a wicked smile spread across those delicious lips. "That can be arranged."

"Good. Because as soon as this festival is over, I'm taking you home where you belong and making you mine, baby."

eight

. . .

IVY

As much fun as the Caribou Creek Christmas Festival was all day—from the hot chocolate to the sleigh ride down Main Street, to the tree lighting ceremony—I'm so happy to be home with Luke. *Home.* Could I really …

Really, Ivy. Your sisters have been so much easier to convince than you.

I turn in a full circle, fully expecting Grandma Annie to materialize. The voice was so loud and clear. Either I'm losing my mind or I need to take a serious break from marathoning my favorite movie. It's probably an unhealthy obsession anyway.

"You okay?" Luke asks, helping me out of my coat at the front door.

"Um, yeah."

After he's hung my coat on a hook, he pulls me back against his chest. His hot breath tickles my neck. "Are you sure, baby? Because if this isn't what you want, tell me now.

Tell me before I plunge my cock inside you and ruin you for every other man. You'll belong to me. You'll be mine and *only* mine."

His possessive words, spoken in a low rumble against my ear, have my inner thighs dripping with need. No one has ever made me feel the way Luke has. I think I probably knew he was the one three years ago. It's why I ran. But I don't know how any of this works. Not when I have a job waiting at a top family law firm pending my bar exam score. A firm that helps hundreds of families in need every year. Would working at Art's firm really be fulfilling enough for me? And how would I feel living this far away from my family?

"Ivy, it's time for you to get out of your own head." His hands slide from my shoulders, cupping my breasts with a playful squeeze. "Let me help you."

"Okay."

Luke leads me to the bedroom where he slowly strips away my clothes. Each layer he peels away is a form of seduction. The way his fingertips drag across my hot skin. The molten lava in his eyes as he drinks in my body. Any insecurity I may have felt about my curves vanishes when he sheds his jeans. The way his cock tents his boxers tells me all I need to know. This man wants *me*. And badly.

I grab his wrist before he can pull down his boxers. "Let me."

Luke watches me slip my thumbs into the waistband of his boxers at either hip and slowly drag them down. His cock catches on the fabric, and I reach inside to guide it free. Wrapping my hand around his massive length. This rod of steel is either going to split me in two or give me pleasure beyond my wildest dreams. My dripping wet pussy doesn't seem worried.

"You like what you see, baby?" Luke asks. His low voice is giving me the best kind of chills.

"Yes." I pull his boxers the rest of the way down, dropping to my knees with a sultry glance upward. At least, I hope it is.

"Ivy," he growls.

"You could sit on the edge of the bed." My voice is shaky, but it's not just nerves. It's anticipation. I've never wanted to suck a man's cock before. But with Luke, I want to watch him lose control at my hand.

He sits on the edge of the bed, moving my hair to one shoulder with his hand as I kneel between his open legs. "I've never done this before," I admit.

"Good. Because mine is the *only* cock your mouth belongs on, baby." If I didn't know Luke the way I do, I might consider this possessive talk a red flag. Hell, I'd tell any of my friends to run. But Luke is familiar. It's like our souls know each other. Why couldn't I just admit it three years ago?

I take him into my mouth, suckling his swollen head. Running my tongue along the rim. He groans in approval.

Luke leans back on his elbows, watching me as I work his cock with my mouth. Taking him in an inch at a time. Running my tongue up and down his shaft. Exploring and tasting all of him. I use my hand to twist the base of his cock as I quicken my mouth. "Fuck, baby," he almost growls. "That feels so good."

I go faster.

Luke springs off his elbows, pulling his dick from my mouth.

"Did I do something wrong?"

"No, baby. You did everything right. And next time, I'll

come in that pretty mouth of yours. But tonight, I'm coming inside your pussy."

He pulls me up from the floor and tosses me on the bed in one quick motion that leaves me a little dizzy. He hovers above me, his hand reaching between my legs. He strokes a finger through my folds.

"So fucking wet."

"So fucking *horny*."

We share a moment of laughter before the sheer need takes over. He rubs circles around my button with this thumb as he slips a finger inside me. "I'm selfish," he says, his dark eyes serious. "I want to fuck you without a condom. But the choice is yours, baby."

"I'm on the pill."

"For now."

Before I can ask what that's supposed to mean, I feel his cock press against my entrance. I've never craved another man the way I do Luke. Hell, sex has never been all that exciting for me. I've never wanted it, craved it, like my girl-friends. There's even been a small part of me that thought, maybe I was broken in that way. His touch melts all my fears, my inhibitions. I know the truth. I've been meant for Luke all along. I spread my thighs wide and push against his cock, inviting him in.

"How do you want it, baby?"

The word "hard" slips out of my mouth unexpectedly. I never thought of myself as that type. But with Luke...

"I'll take you hard and fast this first time, baby. But then, I'm going to spend the rest of the night taking it slow." He lowers his mouth against my ear. "You won't be able to walk tomorrow. Hope that's not a problem."

He plunges inside my channel and my hips buck. The

shock of his massive cock filling me so quickly is almost too much.

"Hey," Luke says, locking eyes with me. "Look at me, baby. I've got you. All you have to do is hold on."

I wrap myself around his hard body and do exactly as he says. I hold on for dear life as he pummels into me. I've never been more turned on in my entire life. Never felt so desired and wanted by another man. The headboard knocks the wall with each powerful thrust. The bed creaks. The symphony of noises we're creating turns me on even more, building the pleasure inside me until I feel ready to burst.

"Luke," I cry out. "Now! It's *now!*"

It feels as though my body is floating as Luke's arms wrap around me tightly. Everything is so fast and intense it's all I can do to keep my strangle-hold on him as every cell in my body explodes in ecstasy. Luke thrusts over and over as my channel convulses around his cock until finally, he stills deep inside me.

I feel his cock pulse as he fills me with his seed. Effectively staking the claim he promised.

"You're mine, Ivy. *Only* mine."

nine

. . .

LUKE

Ivy and I sleep late into the morning and beyond, both of us exhausted from our all-night love making. After I fucked her good and hard, I spent hours worshiping every inch of her body. Slowly bringing her to climax multiple times. There is nothing on this earth sexier than the noises she makes when I take her over the edge of that pleasure cliff.

I love her.

I knew I loved her three years ago.

I knew I loved her the moment I first spotted her sitting behind the reception desk in Art's firm. My entire world changed that day.

"Do you know what time it is?" Ivy asks with a yawn as she starts tracing lazy circles across my chest.

I reach for the phone on my nightstand, unsurprised by the number of unread messages and missed calls. I'll have to check in with Art about dinner tonight. Maggie's urgent texts seem more concerned about me being in hibernation than anything else. "It's almost noon."

Ivy sits up quickly, untangling our legs. "Oh no!" She tosses the covers aside and hops up.

"What's wrong, babe?" I drag my gaze up and down her body without apology. Every inch of her has been kissed, licked, or touched in the past several hours. I've memorized it all.

"I have a Skype call with my sisters! I need your Wi-Fi password."

"Ivy Carol."

She narrows her eyes at me. "I don't have time for a quickie, Luke. Holly's already pissed at me for missing this holiday at home. I can't miss the call too. What's your password?"

"Ivy Carol. That's my password."

That stops her from scurrying around the room, collecting mismatched clothes. A look of love fills her eyes. "It is?"

"What else would it be?"

She pulls one of my t-shirts over her head before kneeling onto the bed, stealing a quick but thorough kiss. "We're talking about this after my call." I pull her in for one more, sliding my tongue into her mouth. Only when she moans do I set her free.

The moment Ivy rushes out of the room, my stomach decides to growl in objection. Apparently, I can't live on sex alone. Though, when it comes to Ivy, I wouldn't mind trying.

ten

. . .

IVY

"Art, that dinner was amazing," I say as I help clear away the dishes. Luke told me that every Christmas Eve, Art makes a traditional Christmas feast to honor his late wife. This year, he made most of it at Luke's house.

We had a long pillow talk last night into early this morning where Luke admitted the decorations are starting to grow on him. His hatred of Christmas is no longer so strong. It's nearly gone.

"We can take care of the dishes, Art," I insist.

Art shoos me out of the kitchen. "I've always done the dishes. Not about to give up that tradition now. You two go enjoy the tree. Watch out for the mistletoe!"

Luke tugs me into his arms, wrapping me in his embrace. I still haven't figured anything out, but I feel less stressed about operating without a plan right now. Winging it. Maybe that's what I really needed all along. I wait for Grandma Annie to chime in, but I don't hear anything now.

I'm going to tell Luke I love him.

"Let's go find that mistletoe," I say to him after stealing a soft kiss. One that hopefully doesn't make Art blush. I take his hand and lead him into the living room, relieved that he's no longer demanding I take down the Christmas tree. In fact, I think his grumpiness toward my favorite holiday has faded almost entirely.

We find the mistletoe hanging in a corner tucked away from the kitchen's sightline. Our lips come together over and over, the need between us growing. I won't rush Art home, but I'll be happy when I have Luke all to myself. Best Christmas Eve ever.

Luke's hand is up my shirt fondling a breast when my phone rings. I'm tempted to ignore it, but that ring is reserved for my bestie.

"You're lucky we still have adult supervision," Luke growls into my neck. "Answer your call. It's Christmas Eve."

I answer on speaker phone because I plan to introduce Luke. I might as well start prepping everyone now that I may not be staying in Denver. I wasn't quite ready to tell my sisters on our call, but I will soon. By New Year's Eve for sure. "Hey Sara!"

"Did you get your results?" she asks, her tone very excited.

"I don't know."

"You haven't checked?"

Luke looks at me curiously. "I've been a little busy. Listen, I want to tell you something—"

"I can't put this in writing, but Daniels, Daniels, and McMullen are going to make you an offer. I may or may not have some insider information. I may or may not have slept with Daniels Junior."

"Wait, what?"

"Check your email, girl! Your biggest dream is about to come true. Merry Christmas! Text me your flight itinerary so I know when to pick you up from the airport tomorrow. Gotta run." The phone goes silent. I feel Luke's intense stare boring into me. His entire body has tensed.

"Your biggest dream?" Though his words are cold, I sense the hurt in them.

I'm not going to lie to Luke. He deserves to know what I'll be giving up. But I've already had a chat with Art. I'd have to retake the bar for Alaska, but he's willing to bring me on and make me partner before he retires. Caribou Creek is no Denver. But there are still plenty of families in need. "They're the biggest family law firm in Denver. It's been my dream job to work for them for years."

"You're leaving."

"Luke, I—"

"You're leaving *tomorrow*." When I reach for him, he steps back. The rejection stings more than I expected. It's a misunderstanding. One I'll have cleared up in a couple minutes if he'd just listen.

"I knew this was a mistake."

I glare at him. "Don't say that."

He looks at the Christmas tree with disgust. "There's a reason I don't celebrate Christmas. This comes down tonight."

Now I'm just pissed. I could pack up my suitcase and sleep in my car until daybreak. Drive to Anchorage and catch my afternoon flight and never look back. But I'm not backing down this time. I'm not running.

"No."

"It's my fucking house. The tree is coming down."

"What's going on in here?" Art asks, approaching cautiously.

"Nothing," Luke grumbles.

"It's not *nothing*," I argue.

"You're right," he says, his eyes shooting daggers at me. "You don't know what it's like to lose your mom at Christmas."

My heart plummets into my stomach and tumbles all the way to my toes. He may as well have punched me in the gut. I've done a pretty damn good job of handling Christmas without Mom for the first time. Until now. Until the harsh reminder. My desire to stay and fight until the lug lets me talk has died.

"Guess it's better I found out now." My heart cracks in two as I march down the hall to pack my suitcase. I'm going home.

eleven

. . .

LUKE

"I always knew you were a little thick when it came to women, but this is a new low even for you." Art's disapproval is strong in both his stern tone and narrowed eyes. It's rare the man is ever upset, much less angry.

But I'm angry too.

Ivy had a dream job lined up this whole fucking time. She was *never* going to stay. So why the hell did she come? If I'd known she was only here for a fling, I would've stayed away until she left. I didn't take her for the kind of woman to use a man. "She lied to me."

"About what?" Art folds his arms over his chest, challenging me to prove him wrong.

"She didn't tell me about the job waiting for her back in Denver."

"Did you ever *ask* her?"

Fuck. I scrub a hand over the back of my neck, pointing my head toward the floor so Art can't see the embarrassment on my face. I feel like a kid getting scolded for doing something fucking dumb and careless.

"Or did you just assume she didn't have a life to get back to?"

"I—"

"Maybe the same way you assumed she didn't know what it was like to lose a parent."

"What are you talking about?"

Art narrows his eyes at me even more. It's a terrifying look for an eighty-three-year-old man. Especially pointed at me. "You should *ask* her." He pokes me in the chest hard. Something Aunt Helen used to do. It would make me smile if this situation weren't so damn tense. "You're not the only one who's lost someone, boy."

I look over my shoulder to the hallway, feeling pulled toward Ivy. Hell, I felt that the second she stormed away.

"If you don't get your ass moving, I'll make sure Santa fills your stocking with coal, young man."

Because this time I am going to laugh, I spin on my heel and walk away before he can call me out. I'm at the bedroom door before I realize I have no fucking clue how to fix the mess I just made. I don't dare look back at Art, though. I can feel those narrowed eyes drilling me with fire beams.

"Ivy?"

"Go. Away."

"Ivy, I'm sorry." I twist the knob slowly, daring to go into my room. Ready to dodge anything that might get thrown at me. She has every right to be mad. "I'm sorry for what I said."

Her narrowed eyes are even scarier than Art's. "What part?"

"All of it. If you really want your dream job, I'm not

going to ask you to stay. I felt blindsided. You never told me."

"You never—"

"—asked. I know." Cautiously I approach her, relieved when she doesn't shrug from my touch. "I've always known you were it for me, Ivy. And when you came back into my life, I thought I was hallucinating. But there you were shaking that very fine ass in front of the Christmas tree I never wanted. The idea of losing you all over again—"

"I want to stay."

"You do?"

"I was trying to tell you. Yes, that's my dream job. But it's not the only family law firm I can work at that will make a difference in people's lives. There's one much closer." Her eyes soften, giving me hope that I haven't completely ruined this with a few careless words. "Art offered me a job. A real one. Partner in a year."

"Really? He never told me."

"I asked him not to so *I* could." Her lower lip trembles, a hasty swallow prefacing a softly uttered, "Jackass."

I want to take her into my arms and never let her go, but I have one more thing to apologize for. "I'm sorry for what I said about my mom. That wasn't fair either."

"No, it wasn't. I lost my mom, too." Her eyes shine with unshed tears, leaving me feeling lower than low. In that moment I know I will never allow my fear to cause her pain again. I'm never going to shut her out or be the asshole who wants her to take down a Christmas tree. I'm going to spend the rest of my life proving I'm worthy of her love.

"I'm so sorry, baby. I didn't know." I wrap her in a tight hug and hold her close for several long, silent beats. I feel her tears soak my shirt. I'll stand here all night holding her if that's what she needs.

"My mom loved Christmas," she admits. "I hear yours did too."

"She did."

"Then let's make sure we honor their memories every Christmas, okay?"

"Baby, if you're willing to give me every Christmas, I promise to make sure we celebrate it however big you want to. I love you, Ivy. I'm going to spend every day from here on out proving it to you. But I only want you to stay in Caribou Creek if it'll make you happy."

"It will."

"You're sure?"

"Yes. Because being without you is miserable. My home is with you."

"And your sisters?"

"They've never been to Alaska. Guess they'll have a reason to visit now."

A gentle knock on the door stirs us from our moment. "I'm heading home," Art announces. "Before you two get too carried away with making up. This old man can only take so much. Breakfast is at nine tomorrow, so don't stay up too late. Or do. You're both young."

The second I hear the front door close, I turn to Ivy and cup her cheek. Tilting her head up toward me. "I'm ready to get carried away if you are."

One corner of Ivy's mouth lifts wickedly. "Why are we still dressed? Better get to work unwrapping your present."

epilogue

. . .

A few days later...

IVY

After triple checking my packing list, I finally zip up my suitcase. It's fuller now than it was when I impulsively hopped on a last-minute flight to Alaska. Now it's filled with gifts for my sisters. I hope they won't mind that I'm a few days late on Christmas presents. At this point, I think they're just happy I'm coming home at all.

The hiss of the shower cuts off, and my heart flutters.

Luke is coming to Denver with me to meet my sisters. To be there when I tell them in person I'm moving to Alaska. I know if they meet him, they'll understand I'm not going off the rails anymore. They'll be supportive of my happiness and of this new chapter. I've signed up to take the bar exam in Alaska, Art has already given me a job, and Luke spent our non-naked time these past few days reconfiguring his closet to include me.

My future is here in Caribou Creek. With Luke. I have an entire checklist to prove it.

Luke stands in the bathroom doorway, a towel wrapped low on his hips. A few stray water droplets glisten off his hard muscles. The urge to lick each and every one is strong. "We have a flight to catch," I say in warning.

"We're early, baby," Luke says, strutting into the bedroom. It takes all of two strides for the towel to fall of its own accord. My gaze unapologetically drops to his cock standing at attention and I shiver in anticipation. Over the past few days, we've spent more time naked than dressed. That cock has made me see stars over and over again.

"I like being early," I say, though my rebuttal is weak at best. The man is standing close enough to me that I feel the heat radiating from his freshly showered skin. The tip of his cock brushes my belly, making me wish I was already naked.

Luke drags his fingers gently beneath my jaw, tipping my face up. My lips part automatically, desperate for his kiss. "We'll be on time, baby. I promise."

"You're all packed?" Even as I ask the question, I drop onto the bed in surrender. I pull my shirt over my head and crawl backward. When I undo the button of my jeans, Luke tugs them off.

"I packed everything on the list."

Hotter words have never been spoken. "Everything?" I practically pant the question.

"Everything."

He climbs up my body until his lips hover above mine. I grip his neck with both hands and tug him down to my mouth. Kissing this man never gets old. Our lips move in a familiar, hungry rhythm. Our tongues swirl and slide together as his body lowers against mine. I feel his erection press into my stomach.

I reach between us and fist his massive length.

Luke groans in approval. "I fucking love your hand on my cock."

As I stroke him, my panties seem to disappear on their own. I don't question how they came off because the only thing I care about is getting this man inside me once more before we're stuck on a plane for several hours. I guide him to my entrance and spread my thighs wider in invitation.

Luke pushes into me slowly. An inch more with each gentle thrust.

"We're going to be late if you keep this up," I moan, wishing we had all day to enjoy each other.

"There are other flights."

I glare at him, and he laughs that low, gravelly chuckle that makes him even sexier.

"Kidding, baby." He presses his lips to mine, hard this time. I tug on his bottom lip with my teeth before he pulls away and sits back on his thighs.

His strong hands scoop beneath my ass and lift. One at a time, he takes my legs and moves them to his shoulders. I'm a mixture of scared and thrilled because I know with my legs straight up in the air like this, the pleasure will be very intense. I grip the sheets half a second before his hands slide to my hips. It's the last gentle move.

Luke's fingers dig into my hips as he greedily slams into my channel over and over. My entire body comes alive with sensation. It's almost too much. A pleasure overload *before* an orgasm. I feel like I'm falling. I squeeze my eyes shut.

"Open your eyes, baby," he orders. "I want to you to be looking right at me when you come."

"Luke—"

"I got you, Ivy. I'll never let you fall."

With that final promise, he pummels into me with force that nearly makes me blind with pleasure. I hold on because I know he'll never let anything bad happen to me. He'll always be there. It's that thought that finally sends me over the edge of the cliff. I come hard. My body explodes from the inside out, like magical confetti.

Luke thrusts one, two, three final times and stills. Emptying his cock inside me.

"When we get back from Denver," he says in a low growl, hands still on my ankles, "We're talking about this birth control thing. Because one of these days, Ivy, I'm putting a baby in you."

Happiness bursts inside my chest at those words. "You promise?"

"I want to build a life with you. A future. A family. I love you, Ivy."

"I love you, too, Luke. I love you so much."

Best. Christmas. Ever.

❄

Read more from Kali Hart!
Click here to subscribe to her newsletter and get a free read.

holly and the ghost of christmas present

Kate Tilney

one

. . .

HOLLY

Ending the call, I stare at my phone in disbelief.

Ivy, my older-than-me-by-ten-minutes sister, is apparently—and inexplicably—in Alaska. Not only that, but tomorrow morning I'm driving my younger-than-me-by-ten-minutes sister Merry—or Mere for short—to the airport so she can attend a wedding in Vermont.

Meanwhile, I'm standing outside a parking garage in downtown Denver trying not to freeze my toes off.

And it's December 21st.

The unimaginable is happening. For the first time in our twenty-seven years on Earth, the Carol triplets will be celebrating Christmas on their own. Oh, I know it's perfectly normal for most adult siblings to spend the occasional holiday alone.

Not us. Christmas is our thing. It's always been our thing.

I mean, our mom was so obsessed with everything Christmas, she named her miracle triplets Ivy, Holly, and Merry.

Now they're leaving me. Not that I can blame them for wanting to be anywhere but here this Christmas. It's our first one without Mom. We lost her suddenly six months ago, and... It's been hard.

Still, I thought we were moving on with our lives. I thought we were getting to a place where we could be okay just the three of us. I guess... I was wrong.

So wrong, I assumed we'd all be in a good enough place to celebrate our mom's favorite holiday together. Just like old times.

A fresh, raw wave of grief fills my chest, and my bottom lip quivers. I catch it with my teeth and take a deep breath in through my nose.

It's going to be okay. At least I have my job. And at least I have our office Christmas party. We hold it every Christmas Eve. I know spending Christmas Eve with your co-workers sounds lame at best and pathetic at worst. But it's actually a lot of fun. And since I took over planning duties a few years ago, the annual Christmas Eve parties have kind of become ragers.

I have reasons to suspect this particular party to be especially exciting.

Ike Noble, the owner of Noble Outwear, who is my boss and mentor, is retiring in the new year. He hasn't officially announced who will be his successor, but he's given plenty of hints that I'll be very happy with what he's decided. He's dropped just as many hints that he'll make a big announcement at the party.

I'm no mind reader, but I don't think it's a stretch to make the connection. Why else would he have been grooming me to take his job for the past couple of years if he didn't plan to choose me?

The thought of seeing "HOLLY CAROL, CEO" on the door to the big corner office immediately erases my melancholy.

Yes, Christmas is going to look very different this year. But with so much to look forward to in the future, that doesn't mean it has to be blue. I just have to get through this month, and I'll have so much to look forward to in the new year.

With that, I turn on my heels and make my way back to the Noble Outwear office. As I walk, I mentally redecorate my new office. It has floor to ceiling windows and a view of the mountains. Maybe I could pick furniture in muted bluish gray tones so it'll match the mountains when they're at their snow-capped and most beautiful.

I'm so caught up in my thoughts, I nearly run into an older woman ringing a bell outside of the building.

"Oh." I stop myself just short of taking her—and the red bucket she's holding—out. "I'm so sorry."

"That's okay, sweetie." She flashes me a bright smile that seems to light up her whole face, and her blue eyes sparkle. For a second, I feel like I've met her before. "You must be in a hurry to get where you're going."

"Yeah, well." I catch myself staring at her for a few moments longer than I should. It's hard to explain, but there's something so familiar about her. She... almost looks like Rose Nylund from *The Golden Girls*.

That must be where I'm getting that feeling of déjà vu.

"It's still no excuse to run into people." I glance at the sign next to her bucket. "You're raising money for the local shelter?"

"That's right. It's so wonderful to be able to pass on blessings, especially this time of year."

"It is." I instinctively dig into my purse and pull out the few dollar bills I have. I wish I had more cash on me. "Here, this is all I have. But will you be around for a while? I'd like to give more."

"Don't worry." Those sparkling eyes of hers flicker a little. "You'll see me again."

I give her a little nod, that strange feeling still brewing inside of me. Shaking it off, I climb into the elevator.

When I reach my floor, my Spidey senses tingle once again. Only this time, it's on account of the atmosphere of the office. Something is happening. Something big. There's a light murmur of hushed whispers and the air practically sizzles with energy.

I pause at my assistant's desk right outside of my office.

Linda, my trusty assistant, is listening closely to Diane, who works in HR. "Rumor has it Ike wants to hand him the reins of the company."

My back straightens, and I'm not quite fast enough to keep the frown from forming on my lips.

"No, that can't be," Linda shakes her head. "His son hasn't been around in years, and Mr. Noble says he's retiring in the new year. There's no way he can possibly catch him up on everything."

"It's called nepotism, honey. It doesn't usually make sense." Diane rolls her eyes and sighs. "It's a good thing Baby Noble is good-looking. Because he's going to be a pain in our ass."

"Ugh, tell me about it." Linda's face scrunches up and she pinches the bridge of her nose. "I swear, I'm getting a migraine already just thinking about it. He'll have so many questions."

"Stupid questions. And we'll have to grin and bear every single one of them."

"Without letting him know we really want to staple Post-Its to his forehead."

"No." Diane shakes her head. "He's way too pretty to staple anything to that forehead of his. No matter how much we might want to flick his nose."

"I wouldn't call him pretty." Linda strokes her chin. "More rugged."

"Tall and handsome. Manly."

"Like the Brawny guy."

They trail off when they see me standing near them. Linda covers the keyboard with her fingers and Diane straightens.

"Good afternoon, Ms. Carol." Linda's smile is just a little too bright. "Did you finally get a hold of your sister?"

"I did." It's on the tip of my tongue to remind her to call me Holly, but my mind is now otherwise engaged. I shift my weight from one foot to the other, trying not to let the tension inside of me grow even more. "Any messages while I was out?"

"Mr. Noble would like you to stop by his office as soon as you can."

I give a short nod as I pass her my coat and purse before heading across the floor to his corner office. There's no way what Linda and Diane have said is true. If Mr. Noble was planning on leaving the company to his son next month, he would have brought him back into the fold much sooner.

His son is probably here for other reasons. Like, to spend the holidays. He's never done that before in the years I've worked here, but maybe this is the exception.

I don't have to worry about losing out on my promotion. Spine straight and shoulders back, I knock on Mr.

Noble's door and push it open, ready to see the real-life Brawny man who most definitely isn't here to poach my job.

two

. . .

JONAS

When my dad's number two walks into the office, it's like a punch to the gut. In more ways than one.

Dad and I were heavily embroiled in another one of our pissing matches. It's not unexpected given our relationship through the years, particularly in the last few. Let's just say, there's a reason I turned down his job offer when I graduated college more than a decade ago. And there are lots of reasons why I've seldom been back to Denver since.

I was doing my best not to listen too closely to what he was saying. I wasn't paying attention when the door to his office swung open. And the handle hit me squarely in the junk.

"Fuck," I hiss under my breath, folding over as the sharp pain flows through every inch of my body.

"Watch your mouth," Dad responds, with a narrow-eyed glare that I'm only just able to see through blurry eyes. "There's a lady present. Speaking of, Jonas, this is Holly."

Still fighting to win the battle over hurling, I clench my jaw and straighten as best as I can. It's time to face the woman my dad has been talking up for several years, usually with a few digs directed at me.

I begin the slow gaze up from her feet. Past a pair of shapely legs and hips on display thanks to a form-fitting pair of jeans. Past an equally full chest accentuated by a bright red sweater. Finally landing on her face.

That's when the second gut-punch strikes.

Holly Carol, quite simply, is one of the most striking women I've ever seen. Striking. That's not a word I've used before outside of talking baseball with my buddies at a sports bar. But the word fits.

She's striking. And stunning. And currently scowling at me even though there's a smile firmly planted on her lips.

Her fuck-me red lips.

Narrowly avoiding a wince, I straighten to my full height and offer her a hand. "It's nice to finally meet you."

Thank God. My words only came out a little pinched.

A spark flickers in her green eyes as she shakes my hand, sending a jolt of warmth straight to my gut. "Finally?"

"My dad has been telling me so much about you."

He didn't mention she was gorgeous. Then again, if he had, I'd probably have to kick the old man's ass. It's bad enough he's decided to propose to his long-time secretary. If he was sniffing around his Senior Vice President of Business Development too...

"Has he?" Holly tugs her hand from mine.

I slide my thumb across my fingers. They're still tingling from her touch. "He said you've single-handedly kept Noble Outwear relevant these past few years."

"I wouldn't say single-handedly did anything." Her lips

twitch, and I swallow hard, my throat suddenly dry. "We have a great team here."

"A team you've been instrumental in building." Dad rounds his desk to rest a hand on Holly's shoulder. "It's been nice having a second in command I can count on. Especially since you went out on your own."

Leaving his whole plan of succession in flux.

My jaw ticks. Of course, Dad would choose to continue our disagreement in front of an audience. And, of course, he'd make me out to be the villain in our situation.

I wonder how much he's told his protege about what happened between us. I wonder why I care.

"I haven't heard much about you," Holly says.

"There's not a lot to say."

Dad snorts. "I guess I shouldn't take it personally that I don't know much about what you're up to these days. Besides dodging calls from your dad."

I breathe in deeply through my nose. I'm not going to let him drag me into a fight. Not in front of her.

"I've been busy with work," I say. "There's not much more to say than that."

Dad looks like he might have something to say about that—like how I should have been busy helping him run the company with our family name in it.

But Holly, either sensing the escalation of private family drama or eager to move this conversation along, speaks first. "So, are you in town for the holidays?"

I share another icy look with Dad. "You could say that."

Somehow, I get the impression she isn't crazy about that answer. There's no other explanation for why her nostrils are flaring.

"Holly always spends the holidays with her family,"

Dad says with more implication in his words. "She's one of a set of triplets."

I arch an eyebrow. "You mean there are three of you?"

She gives me an overly bright, and definitely fake, tight smile. "That's how triplets usually work."

My lips twitch. "Identical?"

"Mostly."

God have mercy. That means there are three breathtakingly stunning women walking the face of the Earth. Each of them sent to tempt mere mortals like me. Then again, given the way she's been scowling at me through a smile for the past several minutes—and the handful of well-placed barbs—maybe they weren't sent from heaven.

That possibility makes me grin. And grimace as my still-sore cock twitches.

"So you must have big plans for the holidays I say." I cringe inwardly. I suck at small talk.

"Actually my sisters will be gone this year." She gives a tight-lipped smile. "It'll just be me."

Now I feel like even more of a dick. "Sorry."

She lifts a shoulder and turns to my dad. "Was there something I can help you with, Mr. Noble?"

"Actually, I was hoping you might let my boy here shadow you the next couple of days. Show him around. Introduce him to people." He gives me a stern look that still has the power to make me feel thirteen years old instead of thirty-three. "Don't be afraid to put him to work with the holiday party."

"Oh, that's not necessary." She tightens her hold on the phone gripped in her hands. "Everything is pretty much ready to go."

"We both know you're going to stay late the night before the party to decorate and transform this place into Santa's workshop. You always do." Dad chuckles. "Have Jonas help you with some of the heavy lifting. Send him on errands."

"Well..."

"It's okay," I say. "You can put me to work. I'm glad to help."

Glad might be a stretch, but I wouldn't say no to spending a little more time with this woman. Something about her... She's striking in every sense of the word.

"Alright, I appreciate your help." She glances at the door. "Was there anything else I can help you with?"

"That'll be all Holly," Dad says.

"I'll see you around."

She gives a short nod in response to me and leaves, pulling the door closed behind her.

"Her mom passed away earlier this year," Dad says. "It was unexpected."

"Oh." I stare at the closed door, feeling like shit about bringing up the fact that she'll be alone this Christmas. "It's hard to lose a parent."

An experience I, unfortunately, know too well.

"Is her dad—"

"He's not in the picture. She's a good girl, though, and won't complain." Dad gives me a hard look. "She knows how important it is to appreciate the family you have."

I sigh and rub my forehead. "Dad, it was never about—"

"I know, I know." He holds up his hands. "You needed space to be your own man." He shoves his hands in his pocket. "I really hope you'll take what I've said under consideration. There's been a Noble running the company since your great-grandfather founded it."

Though we hadn't been in the outerwear business then.

"I will think about it." There's one thing giving me real

pause right now. It's not the years I've been away. I've spent that time getting an MBA and salvaging three companies that were about to go under with my accounting skills. "What about Holly?"

"What do you mean?"

"As your second in command these past few years, don't you think she'll be expecting the job?"

"I've never promised her anything. She'll understand it's a family matter."

I'm not so sure he's right about that. Not if the fire she showed in her eyes earlier was any indication.

"Listen." Dad clears his throat. "Joyce is hoping you'll come over for dinner on Christmas."

Joyce. My dad's personal secretary. His very personal secretary. The woman he started dating mere months after my mom passed away. The woman he plans to marry after his retirement.

I suppose it's time I got used to it—to them.

"Yeah," I say at last. "I'll be there."

three

. . .

HOLLY

"It's the most wonderful time, of the—"

I flip off the car radio before Andy Williams belts out the virtues of the Christmas season. From the passenger seat, Mere gives me a curious look.

"What?" I ask, pushing my sunglasses up the bridge of my nose.

"You skipped the song."

I shrug off the comment. "I'm not in the mood."

Given the way my life has turned upside down during the past twenty-four hours, I'd say I'm well within my rights to not be in the mood for all things Christmas.

She scoffs. "You? Not in the mood for Christmas music?"

"Is that so weird? They've been playing the damn stuff non-stop since Halloween."

"And normally you love it."

She's right. Most years, I'm one of those over-the-top

Christmas people. We all are. We're the kind who put our Christmas trees up before Thanksgiving. We have closets overflowing with ugly festive sweaters. I've even perfected a recipe for eggnog pancakes.

But now… Nope. I'm done with Christmas this year. Just as soon as I make sure the Noble Outerwear Christmas Eve party is the best one ever.

"Is something wrong?" she asks.

"Why would anything be wrong?"

"If nothing was wrong, you wouldn't have said that through gritted teeth."

"I said nothing was wrong, which means nothing is wrong."

Mere arches an eyebrow that says more than words could. "Methinks the lady doth protest too much."

That's the problem with being a triplet. You almost never get anything past your sisters. You're too in-tuned with each other's mannerisms and thoughts to miss anything.

I frown at Mere. "I didn't think you liked Shakespeare."

"Shakespeare? What does he have to do with anything?"

I snort. "Who do you think said that?"

"I'm pretty sure I heard someone say it on an episode of *Gilmore Girls*."

"Wow." I roll my eyes. "You're so cultured."

"I know, right."

I open my mouth to say something else but clamp it shut. Even though she isn't here with us, I can practically hear Ivy scolding us for bickering.

But Ivy isn't here. That makes me the senior-ranking Carol sister. As the senior ranking Carol sister, it's my responsibility to put a stop to the bickering.

I sigh but say nothing, wiggling the fingers I have gripped around the steering wheel.

Giving a satisfied smirk, Mere leans back in her seat. "Look, I know you're upset about Ivy and I being gone for Christmas."

"That's not it."

"Then what's the problem?"

I'm tempted to tell Mere everything that's going on, but I can't quite bring myself to do it. I know she already feels bad enough about leaving me only a few days before Christmas. Especially with Ivy gone on her mystery trip. There's no way I'm going to make her feel even worse by telling her that the promotion I've been working so hard to get is going to be handed to my boss's son.

My boss's son who, despite being a big blip in my plans for the future, is way too easy on the eyes. I shift uncomfortably in my car seat remembering the way his dark brown eyes had the power to make every inch of my body heat up under his stare.

Which... is great. Exactly what I need at the moment. Merry freaking Christmas to me.

"It's just something with the work party," I make up.

Mere nods in understanding. "Don't worry. Whatever it is, I'm sure you'll make it work. You're too stubborn to let it be anything but perfection."

"Gee, thanks." I roll my eyes. "Anyway, enough about that. Do you have your bridesmaid's dress?"

"Yep."

"And a change of underwear?"

She opens her mouth, but quickly clamps it shut. Her brow knits together, and I grit my teeth even tighter. How could someone not remember whether or not they packed underwear before jetting off halfway across the country?

Instantly, my foul mood vanishes, and I have to bite back a laugh.

"I'm sure I packed some," she says a little too defensively.

"Let's hope so." I pull up in front of the departures terminal and put the car in park. "Because you have a flight to catch. If you need anything—"

"I know." She covers one of my hands on the steering wheel. "I'll call. You can do the same for me."

I release the steering wheel and throw an arm around Mere. "Have a good trip."

"I will." She squeezes me back. "Now, try to have a little fun while I'm gone."

That's not likely, but I keep the thought to myself. "I hope you find your underwear."

❄

Unfortunately, my premonition of what awaits me once I get to Noble Outerwear is proven true. As per Mr. Noble's request, his son spends the day trailing me while I introduce him to people and explain what everyone is working on.

Never sparing anyone so much as a smile, he asks short, nosey questions that would piss me off if they weren't so astute.

Even though he's stealing my promotion out from under me, I try to make small talk with him. It doesn't work. Instead, he keeps staring at me intently. It's almost as if he's picking me apart to find all of my flaws so he can use them against me to secure the promotion.

He even turned down my offer to bring him a peppermint mocha back from the coffee shop. I mean, seriously?

What kind of person frowns when you offer him a cup of deliciousness?

It appears someone else is lacking in Christmas spirit this year, too.

By the time I get home that evening, I have a splitting headache and a desperate need for some spiked eggnog. I may be over Christmas this year, but it would be a waste to let the cartons I've already bought go bad.

This is the same mindset I have when I stay up half the night stress-baking copious amounts of sugar cookies. They're my mom's recipe and baking them makes me feel closer to her. At the same time, it makes me miss her and my sisters all the more. So it's a double-edged sword.

By 2 a.m., I've baked and decorated several dozen, going so far as to plate them for sharing at the office, I feel more in control of my emotions. I'm still anxious about what the future holds for me once I get to the office. But at least I'm armed with a bunch of cookies.

A bunch of cookies I'm precariously balancing in my arms as I walk from the parking garage to the office building later that morning.

"Is it January yet?" I mumble when I catch myself before tripping and spilling my delicious cargo.

"Careful there." A pair of strong hands grip me by the elbows.

My spine stiffens and I slowly turn around and come face to face with none other than Jonas Noble. My knees buckle slightly.

"Whoa." He tightens his grip, his dark eyes narrowing. "Are you okay?"

"I'm fine. I must have found a slick spot."

He glances around to look for the spot, and my cheeks

flush anticipating the moment he catches me in a lie. But, he proves to be more of a gentleman than I would guess.

"Yeah, it gets pretty slick this time of year." He releases my elbows. "Will you be okay getting all of those inside?"

"I've got them."

"Are you sure?" Before I can protest, his lips curve into a half-grin that so surprises me, I go silent. "My dad did instruct you to put me to work."

I give a short laugh. "Well, I suppose you could carry some of them."

"With pleasure." He takes the bulk of the boxed up cookies. He draws close enough that I catch a whiff of his masculine scent. It's like a spicy mixture of orange and sandalwood.

He starts to step away and pauses. "Are you coming in?"

"I just need a minute."

He studies me closely for a minute before heading back for the building. Releasing a breath, I wait until he's inside before I follow.

Outside the door, the woman who was ringing the bell the other day is back, armed with her overly cheerful smile.

"Why, hello there again, Holly." Her face crumbles slightly in concern. "You look like you're a little down in the dumps. Is everything okay?"

I open my mouth and pause. "How do you know my name?"

"We met the other day. Don't you remember?"

"I remember." We must have exchanged names. And, darn it all, I can't remember her name. I don't want to be rude and admit it. "Sorry. Mental lapse."

"Oh, I'm familiar with those. When you get to be my age, you have a lot of them. So, tell me. What's going on?"

I want to protest, but something about this woman makes me want to confess everything to her.

I sigh. "This Christmas is turning out to be even harder than I thought it would be. My sisters are both on opposite sides of the country, leaving me alone for the holidays for the first time in my life."

She nods sympathetically. "It's hard to be alone this time of year."

"It was always going to be tough. Our mom passed away earlier this year. She... she loved Christmas. She made it so special."

I blab on about all of the little and big things she used to do to make the holidays extra cheerful for us. "I keep thinking about all of those holidays in the past and wishing I could experience it one more time."

I sigh again. "I thought I could distract myself with my job. I thought I was a shoo-in for a huge promotion. But now someone else is here, and they're probably going to get it. I don't know. My head feels like it's spinning all the time with all of these thoughts of the past and worries for the future. I can hardly keep them all straight."

"Hmm." The bell ringer nods thoughtfully. "If you don't mind my saying, Holly, it sounds like you're so caught up in the memories of your past and your plans for the future. Have you ever tried being more present?"

"Be present?"

"Absolutely. Forget the past. Forget the future. Just... take every moment as it comes and say yes to every opportunity to add some joy to your life."

She smiles at me, and somehow the tension inside of me seems to go away. "It's Christmas, after all. A time for joy. And a time for presents."

four

. . .

JONAS

Going to the Christmas tree lot with Holly was a mistake.

After spending half the night tossing and turning as I had lewd dream after lewd dream about her, being so close to her all day had been hell.

Then I'd accompanied her to the lot, per my father's request, to help her get a tree for the party. That shouldn't have been too bad. Except that Holly, apparently determined to drive me crazy, kept bending over to look at each trunk before she found one that would do the trick.

Every time she bent over, visions of stepping up behind her and seeing if the tree was sturdy enough to hold our weight while I drove us both to satisfaction filled my head.

At least it's fucking cold outside. That, and the long walk back to the offices, does a little to help cool my lust.

Outside the building, Holly freezes suddenly. "Okay, stop."

Unprepared for the sudden halt in motion, I run into the

stump of the tree with an "oof." "A little warning would be nice."

"I said stop."

"After you already stopped."

She waves off my response as if that one crucial fact makes no difference. "Don't change the subject."

"What subject?"

"This." She gestures emphatically at me as if that explains everything.

"What does"—I wave my hands back at her—"this mean?"

"Why are you being so mean to me?"

I frown. "Mean? I just helped you drag a Christmas tree almost a mile across downtown Denver."

"And you glared at me the entire time. Just like you did yesterday."

Her eyes are bright and sparkling. It's all I can do not to stare at them. Especially after she's just accused me of glaring—when I only thought I was staring—all day.

"I'm not glaring." When she rolls her eyes, I take a step toward her and nearly bump into the stump again, but catch myself. Stepping around it, I move toward her. "I promise. I wasn't glaring."

"Then—then why won't you talk to me?"

"I talk to you."

"Barely. You hardly answer my questions." She raises her chin as if she's drawing upon some courage. It seems to me, she has plenty of it. It's one of the things I like about her.

There are a lot of things to like about her.

"It… seems like you hate me."

"No." I shake my head and take another step toward her. "I don't hate you."

"Then—"

"You… you make me nervous," I admit.

Her eyes grow wide. "I make you nervous?"

"You do." I run a hand over the cropped whiskers on my jaw. "Look, you're gorgeous."

"Gorgeous?"

I dart a glance at her, silently asking if she's seriously questioning that fact. She has to know she's stunning. "You're so good at taking command of every situation."

"I take command?"

"You're a force to be reckoned with, Holly. A smart, brilliant, beautiful force. And I can't seem to keep myself from staring, because I'm trying to figure you out."

There. I said it. With plenty of words strung together to form sentences that she shouldn't be able to accuse me of not speaking to her again.

"You want to figure me out?"

I can't help but smirk at the way she's been parroting me. "I apologize if it's made you uncomfortable."

"Well… apology accepted." She picks up her end of the tree. "We should probably get this inside before it's dark."

With a nod, I return to the other side and hoist up the tree by the trunk. "Lead the way."

We manage to get the tree up to the office with only a brief harrowing moment in the elevator, in which I shouted "PIVOT!" about half a dozen times. Fortunately, Holly seemed to find that hilarious.

Once we're in the now-empty Noble Outerwear offices, Holly leaves me briefly to drop her coat and purse off in her office and retrieve the lights and decorations she needs.

When she returns, I have my sleeves rolled up and I give the tree a light shake. "Where do you want it, boss?"

She blinks a few times before frowning. "Don't shake the tree. You'll get needles everywhere."

"No, I won't."

She stalks toward me and pulls the tree aside and points to the ground. "See."

Sure enough, there's a small pool of pine needles.

I lift a shoulder. "I'll clean it up later."

"You better." But her words don't have any heat.

For a while, we wordlessly work together while we get the stump in the stand.

"Wait," I say before she goes to get a razor so we can cut the twine and release the branches. "Let me get a picture of you."

She arches an eyebrow. "You want a picture of me?"

"With the tree. I'll send it to my dad. So he can see I'm being helpful."

"Shouldn't you be in it too?"

I lift a shoulder. "Sure."

I stand next to her, posing with the tree between us. I extend my arm and shake my head. "We need to get closer."

Both of us lean toward each other. The hairs on the back of my neck stand up at her nearness. I snap the photo and pull the phone back for us to look at.

Now Holly shakes her head. "Nope."

"What's wrong with it?"

"You aren't smiling."

I roll my eyes but extend my arm again. This time, I plaster the biggest, cheesiest grin on my face, crossing both of my eyes as I do. *Click.*

I show her the photo on the screen. "Better?"

"Much." She smirks. "Come on. We need to get scissors."

"My dad keeps some in his office," which is the closest one to us at the moment.

Though it's not a task that takes two people, we both stride to his office. Not that I mind. It gives me another chance to admire the gentle sway of Holly's hips as she walks in front of me.

"I think your dad keeps a box of utility knives on the shelf behind the door."

Nodding, I close the door so I can reach them. I look through a few boxes before I find it. "Will this one work?"

"I grabbed some scissors too, just in case."

"Then it seems like we should be covered in cutting the twine."

"Seems like it." She grins at me, and I miss a breath.

Holly reaches for the handle. And it—the damn handle that nearly turned me into a soprano the other day—falls off the door in her hand. Her eyes widen and she meets my gaping stare.

"Well, shit," she says with a short laugh.

Panic lances my heart and I cross the short distance to her and take the knob. She stands back and watches, humor playing on those tempting lips of hers, while I try—and fail—several times to get the handle to stick back on it.

"So that won't work." I pass the handle back to her. I turn back toward my dad's desk and grab a ruler. "Let's try this."

She arches an eyebrow. "A ruler?"

I stick it into the small hole, trying to see if I can trigger the handle on the other side. But the ruler is too wide. I try the pair of scissors next. Then my finger.

None of them work.

"So much for that idea." Running my hands through my

hair, I pace back and forth to my dad's office. "We have to get out of here."

There's no way I can stay stuck in here with this woman for God-knows-how-long until we're discovered. Not when every time I look at her my libido lights up like the damn Christmas tree we just hauled up the elevator.

"We should call someone." I pause mid-stride. "Do you have the number for the security desk on your phone?"

"I do, but..." She shakes her head. "I don't have my phone. It's in my purse. Which is in my office. What about your phone?"

I pat my pockets and wince. "I left it next to the tree."

I stalk across the room to my dad's desk. I pick up the phone and there's no dial tone. "How do I dial out?"

"You can't."

"What do you mean I can't?"

I turn, and she's pulling a face. "The phones—and the Internet—are all down tonight for routine maintenance."

"You're joking."

"I wish I was."

I suck in a breath. Great. Just great. I'm stuck in my dad's office with a beautiful woman who apparently finds me frustrating.

Could this Christmas get any better?

five

. . .

HOLLY

"Okay." I take a deep breath, taking command of the emotions churning inside of me so I can get a better grip on the situation. "We have to be calm."

"Calm?" Jonas snorts. "That's your grand plan for how we're going to deal with this?"

"I'd say it's a better start than freaking out and going into a rage. But then again, maybe that's how you do things back in Seattle."

"It's not how we…" Heaving a sigh, Jonas rubs his forehead. "You're right. We need to be calm."

I give him a stern look. "Do we need to do some breathing exercises?"

"I can control myself."

"Good." I glance around the office forming a plan.

If we were going to get stuck anywhere in the Noble Outerwear offices, at least we ended up in Mr. Noble's executive suite. There's a mini fridge in the corner, which I know his secretary/future wife keeps stocked with bottles of water. There's also a private restroom, so we don't have to worry about designating a pee corner if we end up here overnight. Oof. That would be one way to take a bad situation and make it a real nightmare.

"Okay," I say resolutely. "First things first, we need to find a way to let people know we're stuck in here."

"Without working phones?" He scratches the back of his head in agitation. "How do we do that?"

"We make a sign." I race to the filing cabinet where I know we store reams of paper. "We write one letter to a piece of paper, filling in the letters so they're thick and can be seen, and we hang them in the window."

"How are people going to see it? We're on the fourteenth floor."

It's a good point, but we don't have any other choice. "Maybe someone in the hotel across the street will see it."

"Maybe we'll have better luck stomping our feet hoping someone is still in the office below us and calls security."

I glare at him. "It couldn't hurt to try, could it?"

He sighs. "You should draw the letters. I'll color them in. My handwriting sucks."

We each take a seat at Mr. Noble's desk. Jonas insists I take his dad's chair. A seat I've imagined filling many times. Though, realistically, even if I became CEO, I'm sure I'd get my own chair. One with better lumbar support.

We work silently, amassing a small pile of letters.

I peek up at him through my eyelashes, grinning when I see he has his lips pursed in concentration.

"So," I say. "What's your favorite Christmas movie?"

He glances up. "What?"

"If this doesn't work, we'll have a lot of time to kill. I figure we should make some conversation."

He turns his attention back to his paper. "Muppet Christmas Carol."

"Oh, I love that one. Michael Caine is a treasure."

"Yeah." He fills in more of the block. "What about you?"

"There are so many good ones, let's see." I tilt my head to the side. "There's *Miracle on 34th Street* and *It's a Wonderful Life*."

"Both good classics."

"But I guess my favorite is *Elf*. The one where Will Farrel—"

"I know *Elf*." He gives a light grin. "It's a good one."

"Well, my mom knew it was one of my favorites so she always put it in our movie rotation. And one year, to surprise me, she decorated my bedroom the way Buddy decorated his family's apartment."

"With lights and streamers and snowflakes."

"Exactly. She…" I trail off, a huge wave of grief rushing over me. I swallow hard. "She was always so good at making Christmas special for us. It was the best time of year."

"Moms are good at Christmas." He meets my gaze. "But it sounds like your mom was really good at it."

"I… I sometimes wonder if it would have been better or worse if we'd known last Christmas was going to be our last Christmas." I clear my throat to keep a lump from forming, though it desperately wants to. "Would I have made more of a point to savor every moment? Would I have appreciated it more?"

"Or would you have been too sad or so focused on memorizing everything that you didn't give yourself the freedom to be in the moment to enjoy it?"

"Is that what happened to you?"

He nods, clenching his jaw twice. "It was… hard. I tried

so hard to make everything perfect for her. The way she used to always make it so perfect for me. But the more I tried..."

He stares back down at the desk.

"Maybe it is for the best we didn't know then." My bottom lip quivers and I catch it with my upper lip. I give myself a moment to maintain my composure. "Our last Christmas was just like all the others. Happy. Loud. More than a little over the top."

He chuckles lightly at that. "It sounds like fun."

"It was. Mom always made Christmas fun. I only wish…"

I have to stop myself again because the risk of tears is just too strong.

Jonas clears his throat. "I understand."

Suddenly I feel oddly naked. More than naked. If I was naked, Jonas would only have removed the layers of my clothing. Stripping me bare for his eyes to feast upon.

That's a thought that makes my cheeks flush and need pools between my thighs.

But that's not the layer he's pulled away. Somehow, he's managed to take off the cheerful and outgoing mask I wear like armor. He's found the root of the grief I've been carrying with me for the past six months. He's found the fears I have for the future.

He's left me emotionally naked and vulnerable. He knows the deepest secrets of my past and future. Truths only my sisters know.

The bell ringer's words come to mind. *You're so caught up in the memories of your past and your plans for the future. Have you ever tried being more present?*

That advice has never seemed more prudent than now. For tonight, I'd like to forget everything that's weighing me down. Surely there's something we can do to keep ourselves occupied in the present.

Throwing myself at him and shoving my tongue down his throat while my hands explore every inch of his rock-hard body would be one way to accomplish that task. I smirk to myself. Tempting as that would be—and believe me, I've never been so tempted—I'm not sure I can stop worrying about the future to take that step. It would change our workplace dynamics.

They're already changed, a voice whispers.

I shake it off and glance around Mr. Noble's office looking for something that can keep my thoughts focused on less serious things while we're stuck here.

"Anyway." I take a deep breath in quickly and let it out. "What's your favorite Christmas candy?"

He groans, but by the time we finish making our signs and hanging them up in the window, we've fallen into an easy enough conversation, each of us learning more about the other.

We stand back to admire our work. I turn to look at Jonas. "I suppose there's only one thing left for us to do."

He arches an eyebrow and the butterflies in my belly flutter. "What's that?"

I reach for the pile of printer paper and pluck the scissors out of a mug on Mr. Noble's desk. "We find out which one of us is the best at making snowflakes."

six

. . .

JONAS

"How did I let you talk me into doing this?" I grumble as I awkwardly pick up a pair of sewing scissors from a kit in my dad's desk.

I didn't even know my dad knew how to sew, let alone had a sewing kit. According to Holly, my future stepmother signed him up for an introductory sewing class last summer. He wanted to be able to mend the tears he frequently gets in his shirts.

Apparently, Dad was the star pupil in his class. Never mind that the rest of the students were all six and seven.

"He's really proud of the certificate they printed out for him," Holly had said with a light laugh that, for some reason, brought jingle bells to mind. "Joyce has it hanging up on their fridge. Along with the mosaic magnets they made during a class they took last spring."

That's a new title for Ike Noble: Crafter. Guess I can add that to the list of things I didn't know about my old man.

Then again, sending each other an "Are you still alive?" text every couple of months doesn't open itself up for many heartfelt conversations about what you and the other person are doing with your lives.

I sigh, and Holly rolls those dazzling green eyes of hers. "Oh don't act like I'm forcing you to make snowflakes. You can stop any time you want."

"And give you the satisfaction of declaring yourself to be the snowflake-making champion of Noble Outerwear." I scoff good-naturedly. "Think again, buddy."

"Buddy?" She arches an eyebrow and my heart thuds.

"You're right, we're not exactly friends are we?"

Though I'm teasing her, what I said is true. While we may have declared a truce and made ourselves friendlier to each other, that hardly makes us buddies. I'm not sure I could ever really be friends with her. Not when watching her purse those lips of hers makes me want to put them to another use.

I groan inwardly and try to shake the thoughts of those lips wrapped around me out of my head. But it's too late. My cock is already almost painfully hard and throbbing.

Giving another sigh, heavier this time, I try to shift the subject—and my dirty thoughts—back to something safer.

"If we're going to make paper snowflakes, I think it's only fair that we trade off the big scissors and the little scissors for every other snowflake." I shake my already cramping hand. "Otherwise, I may do permanent nerve damage to my fingers."

"It sounds to me like you're making excuses for why I'm going to come out the snowflake-making champion." Her tempting lips twitch. "But in the interest of fairness, I'll consider your request."

"Consider my request?"

"Yes." She raises her chin. "After all, no one said life is fair. Plus, finders keepers, and all that."

I can't resist grinning. "Is that more lessons learned from life as a triplet?"

"One of many." The sparkle in her eyes dims a little.

I can feel my own spirits sink along with her humor. Damn, I can be such a thoughtless ass sometimes. She's already admitted how hard this Christmas is with her sisters out of town and their mom gone. And here I am, poking at her pain. Unintentionally. But I should still be more thoughtful.

She makes a little sound that's part sigh, part something I can't quite put my finger on. "It's more a lesson of being the middle child."

"Does birth order make a lot of difference as a triplet?"

"It makes all the difference, *my friend*." She gives me a teasing look that slices through the brief tension that settled over us. "Even now, it's how we decide everything from who gets to ride shotgun to who gets to open the first and last present on Christmas morning."

"And where does that leave you as the one in the middle?"

"Usually cracking jokes or doing something silly. Like tying my little sister to a chair with Christmas ribbons or sneaking into my big sister's room while she's asleep to hide the outfit she laid out the night before."

"It sounds like you were a bit of a wild child."

"Child? This happened last year." She laughs a little. "Kidding." She wrinkles her nose. "My teachers said I acted out because I wasn't getting enough attention. But that wasn't it. Mom was really good about giving us all one-on-one time. She never let any of us feel left out or like we weren't getting enough time."

"She sounds like a wonderful woman."

"She was the best." She offers me a sad smile. She looks like she wants to ask me something, but doesn't.

"What? You can ask me anything."

"It's pretty personal."

"I think given our current situation, we're past the point of worrying about something being too personal."

"Okay, well, if you change your mind and decide—"

"Just ask the question, Holly."

She clenches her teeth before blurting out, "What happened with you and your dad?"

I flinch, but joke. "See, that wasn't so bad."

"Sorry, was that too rude?"

"No, you're good. It's just… complicated. It might take a while."

"Well, we have nothing but time."

"True." I rub my forehead. "Okay, the short version: I was a mess after my mom died. She'd been sick for a while, so we knew it was coming. But I don't think you can ever be completely prepared for something like that."

She nods, and I know she—of all people—understands the pain of losing a mom.

"I was in my early twenties. My mom was gone. And… I felt like my dad wasn't as upset as I was." I stare down at the paper in my hands. "What I didn't realize then is that my dad and mom had done a lot of their grieving together. Before she was gone. When I found out he was seeing Joyce after mom was only gone a few months…"

Holly places a hand on my forearm. Her silent show of support gives me the strength to continue.

"We exchanged some words. He told me I needed to grow up. I told him he needed to keep it in his pants." I tighten my grip on the paper and it crinkles slightly. "It ended with me saying I needed some space. He could do what he wanted with his company. We've barely been able to have a civil conversation since."

She stares at me intently with those brilliant green eyes of hers. My palms grow sweaty, and I have to tighten my grip on the scissors to keep from letting the slip out of my grasp.

"I know this probably isn't going to be a popular suggestion..." She lifts her shoulders apologetically. "But maybe you should sit down with your dad and have a serious conversation. Let him know how you feel."

"Well, that's the problem, isn't it? We Noble men aren't the best at talking about mundane things. Like football or baseball. Talking about feelings..." I shake my head and turn back to cutting chunks out of the folded paper in my hand. "We'd be in trouble before we started."

"Maybe that's the way it would have been in the past. But you can't worry about the past. Or the future."

"Is that some new-Agey 'be present and mindful' B.S. you picked up in a yoga class?" I scoff and take a few angry cuts at my snowflake. "Because that might work while you're trying to get into downward dog, but it doesn't have the same effect on two stubborn sons of bitches who haven't seen eye to eye... ever."

"Well, at least you're self-aware."

I glance up at her. "Come again?"

"You admit that you're a stubborn son of a bitch." She smiles sweetly. "You're already halfway to achieving that present mindful bullshit."

A pit settles in my stomach, along with a heavy dose of guilt and shame. "I'm also an ass."

"See. I told you. Self-aware." Holly smirks to herself, and I once again find myself struggling to breathe.

What hold does this woman have on me? Forty-eight hours ago, she was little more than a name to me. A name my dad liked to throw out during our rare conversations as a way to make me feel like shit.

Now, she's more than a name. She's Holly, the woman who has somehow found a way to crawl under my skin. The woman who has taken such a hold of me, I can't think straight.

I clocked her as striking from the start. That hasn't changed, but she's even more than that. Sitting with her shapely legs curled underneath her, she's cutting away at her snowflake with as much enthusiasm as she seems to approach everything. Her tongue is sticking out of the corner of her mouth in focus. I wonder if she even realizes she's doing it.

I wonder what her lips and tongue taste like. I bet she tastes like the sugar cookies she baked and the rum we stole from Dad's desk.

Sugar cookies and rum. And Holly.

My cock twitches and I tear my gaze from her in a half-hearted attempt to cool my libido. Short of me hopping into a cold shower or a pile of snow stark naked, there's not much hope of that.

"How did you get to be so wise in the ways of inter-family serious conversations?" I ask, faking interest in my snowflake. "More triplet stuff?"

She grins. "Let's just say I've had some good advice of my own lately from a friend."

"And what kind of advice did you get?"

"She told me... to stop worrying so much about the past or future. To focus on the present."

"That's pretty good advice. Though tough to follow."

"That's what I thought. I—" She flinches and gasps, dropping her scissors and the paper.

"What's wrong?" I drop my own supplies and reach her without waiting for an answer. I see the faint red line of a paper cut on her finger and wince. "Ouch. Those things hurt."

"So bad."

"Hold on." I leave her sitting on the floor and grab a tissue from Dad's desk. When I return, I lower myself next to her on the ground, even closer than before. I carefully grasp her hand in mine again and wrap her finger.

Neither of us says anything for long moments. At her nearness, I can feel my heart thundering in my chest, matching her own pulse, which is beating quickly against my thumb.

"I think the bleeding has stopped," she says at last.

I pull the tissue back and see she's right. On impulse, and remembering her words about living in the future, I lower my head to press a kiss to her finger.

She sucks in a breath and watches me closely. She doesn't pull back and raising my gaze I see it. The flicker of fire in her eyes.

It's all the invitation I need. I pull her into my arms and capture her lips in a searing kiss. The last thought I have before I sink into it is that I was right.

She tastes like rum and sugar cookies.

seven

. . .

HOLLY

Wrapped in Jonas's strong embrace, I let the kiss consume me, allowing myself to sink into it completely.

I don't worry about the past.

I don't think about what this could mean for the future.

For the first time, I think I understand what my bell-ringing friend meant when she said I should focus more on the present. Right now, I'm a big fan of living in the present.

I slide my hands up his chest, stroking the muscles under his flannel shirt. I reach for the buttons, eager to touch his bare skin. Jonas releases his hold on me to grab my hands. He breaks off the kiss and looks down at me.

"Are you sure?"

"Definitely."

"Because this could make certain things complicated." He stares intently at me, passion thick in his dark eyes. "And I don't want—"

"Would you mind if we don't worry about what might

happen tomorrow or what happened yesterday? Could we just focus on what's happening right now?"

His lips, swollen from mine, curve up. "I can do that."

"Good. Then kiss me."

"Yes, boss." A little thrill runs up my spine at his words, and it's heightened by his mouth on mine again.

This kiss is every bit as searing as the first, only there's more to it. It's every bit as urgent, but it's more insistent. It's as if he's silently urging me to feel every bit of joy and desire I can at this moment.

And it's not hard to do.

I return to removing his shirt, splaying my hands over his bare skin once it's revealed.

I suck in a breath. "God, you're so strong."

"It's from carrying that Christmas tree." He grazes his teeth along my jaw and I gasp, clinging to him as a fresh wave of pleasure fills me.

"I should have you carry more trees then."

"Your wish is my command."

He pulls me to the ground, cradling me in his arms as he nibbles his way along the curve of my neck, lower and lower until he reaches my shirt's neckline.

"This sweater of yours has been driving me crazy all day." He reaches for the hem and inches it up bit by bit. "I've been wondering what's underneath it. I've wanted to unwrap you like a present."

"I hope you like what you find."

He pulls back so he can pull the sweater the rest of the way up and tosses it aside. Fire flashes in his eyes and he hungrily explores my body with his gaze.

"It's even better than I imagined." He leans forward and presses his mouth on the edge of my lacy red bra. "Better than any present I've ever found on the tree."

We move against each other. Letting our fingers and lips work their magic. Stroking each other. Teasing. Though we're both clearly wild with desire, we take our time.

After all, it's clear our sign in the windows didn't draw any attention. We have all night to worship each other.

When his fingers and lips find the sensitive spot between my thighs, I swear, I have a religious experience. I move against him, sliding my fingers into this thick dark hair.

"Come for me," he murmurs against my clit before sucking it into his mouth.

It's enough to send me over the edge, the orgasm flowing through my veins and filling every inch of me with pleasure. I'm panting by the time it's over, and still tingling from wanting more.

"I need you inside of me," I say.

He presses his lips to mine. "Give me one second."

He reaches into his long-since discarded jeans and pulls a condom out of his wallet. I take it from him, ripping the foil open and tossing it aside.

As he settles at my side again, I push him to his back. Hovering over him, I lean forward to press a kiss to the tip of his hard length. He sucks in a breath. Grinning, I slide the condom over him.

He takes my hands and helps me straddle his hips. Our stares are locked on each other as he helps to lower me onto his cock, slowly filling and stretching me.

"Oh my God." My eyelids flutter. "Oh my... God."

"You said it." He releases my hands so he can stroke my body. "Fuck, you're gorgeous."

He glides his hands up my belly, stroking my bare breasts. Teasing the already swollen nipples.

"Are you ready?" I ask.

He nods and drops his hands to grip my waist. "Ride me, baby."

And I do. Slowly at first, savoring the feel of him inside of me. Then he changes his hold to grip my ass, helping me find a new angle that helps to build that wickedly delicious sensation inside of me again.

This time, when I can feel myself about to lose control, I hold on, waiting to see if he's ready to join me. He bucks up his hips against me and stares at me, his eyes seeming to stare right into my heart.

The ripples erupt inside of me, and we move together, finding fulfillment in each other. When the last waves of pleasure subside, I collapse against his chest.

Stroking my back, Jonas nuzzles the side of my neck. "Can I just say what a fan I am of living in the present?"

Finding the strength to lift an arm, I stroke his cheek, lightly stroking his whiskers. "You and me both."

※

Sunlight is barely streaming into the windows the next morning when the door to Ike Noble's office swings open, revealing the man himself.

"Dad." Jonas scrambles to his feet and darts a glance my way. I sit up on the floor, where we both curled up last night. Thankfully, we put our clothes back on after so we could stay warm. Well, we put on most of our clothes. I'm not entirely sure where my bra has gone. "What are you doing here?"

"Someone in the building across the way saw your signs." He gestures toward the window we covered in paper last night. "I guess they tried to come in and find you last night, but they miscounted the floors. Security sent an email out to all of the office managers last night."

A dark flash flickers in Jonas's eyes. "And Joyce waited until this morning to say anything?"

"We were at a holiday party last night and got in late. We didn't check our messages until this morning. She told me as soon as she saw it." A fierce frown crosses Mr. Noble's face. "You have to stop thinking the worst of her. She's going to be your—"

"I know. I know." Jonas holds his hands up in surrender and sighs. He looks at me again, and I can read the regret from his outburst. "Sorry, I know Joyce is a… nice woman. I shouldn't have jumped to the wrong conclusion. But… we were stuck in here overnight. We didn't get much sleep last night."

"No." Mr. Noble seems to take a closer look at his office. His stare lasers in on the pile of snowflakes we made. The crumbles leftover from the cookies we ate as our dinner. The empty glasses next to his half-empty bottle of rum. "Though, it looks like the two of you managed well enough."

Then he zeroes in on something on the floor near the desk. I follow his line of sight and wince. There it is. My red lace bra. And… Oh my God. Next to it is the open foil wrapper from the condom we used last night.

I clench my eyes shut, my face burning hot. Oh my God. There's only one thing I can do. Well, two things, really. First, I need to grab my bra and race out of here before I can add to my embarrassment by crying. Second, once I get home and wash off everything that happened in the longest shower ever and wrap myself in the fluffy candy cane-striped robe Mom gave me a few Christmases ago, I'll draft my letter of resignation.

Because there is no way—no way at all—I will ever be able to show my face in this office again.

Goodbye, promotion that was probably not going to happen anyway.

Hello to the big bowl of sugar cookie dough sitting in my fridge.

Unable to stand the tension another moment, I rise to my feet, ignoring the hand Jonas offers to help me rise.

"If you gentlemen will excuse me..." I don't meet either of their stares and—with as much composure as I can—I retrieve my bra and shoes.

Then I race out of the office, ignoring the sound of Jonas calling my name. I can't face him right now.

Not when what happened last night was so prominently on view.

Not when the look on Mr. Noble's face leaves no doubt about what I can expect for my non-existent future with the company I've worked so hard to build up.

Once I'm out the door, I pick up my pace. I pause only long enough to grab my purse, coat, and phone from my office. I slide my feet into my shoes and pull on my coat during the ride down the elevator.

When I step outside, I look around, disappointed to find that a certain bell ringer isn't at her post. Not that I should expect her. It is Christmas Eve. She probably has family and friends to spend the day with.

Unlike me.

The self-pity wraps around me until it's almost suffocating. At least... At least I have a video call with my sisters to look forward to this afternoon. Hopefully, it'll make me feel less alone.

❄

A few hours later, as my sisters' familiar faces fill the phone screen, it's all I can do not to burst into tears.

Instead, I stay uncharacteristically quiet while each of them takes a turn filling us in on the adventures with their trips. It's with more than a little surprise that both of them share their own romantic entanglements. It's only been a few days since we were all together, and yet so much has happened.

When Mere has finished telling us about the man she's been spending time with in Vermont, Ivy turns the conversation toward me.

"You've been oddly quiet, Holly. What's going on?"

"Nothing," I blurt out and wince. I've said it more than a little too quickly.

It doesn't go unnoticed by my sisters.

"Come on, Holly." Ivy gives me a stern look. "Tell us. Everything."

Taking a shaky breath, the words spill out of me. I tell them about the arrival of Jonas and the implication it has on my promotion. I tell them about the major shift in my feelings for him, and how much more they've complicated the situation.

I even admit that I'm feeling lonely, not just alone.

"I've been trying so hard to not let myself dwell on the past or worry about the future," I say, remembering the kindly meant advice from my new bell-ringing friend. "I've been trying to stay in the moment. But, it seems to me, being in the moment is what got me into this mess to begin with."

"But what if it doesn't have to be a mess?" Mere asks.

"My boss knows I had sex with his son. On the floor of his office."

"Well, it'll be your office soon."

I roll my eyes. "You really think he's going to hand his company over to me instead of his son? Especially after…"

I shake my head. I can't relive that moment again. It's too humiliating.

"For what it's worth, I think you should keep living in the moment," Ivy speaks up at last. "You need a break from worrying about everything else."

"Easier said than done."

"It is," she agrees. "But if I've learned anything, it's that you can't let fear keep you from opening your heart. Yes, you risk being heartbroken. But that's better than living your life with regret."

My sister's words resonate in my head long after we end our video call and they go back to their adventures.

Once again, I find myself with two options. I can sit and wallow, wondering what might happen. Or, I can go to the party tonight and find out what awaits me.

I'm not sure which option will leave me with fewer regrets.

eight

· · ·

JONAS

Holly disappears through the door at lightning speed. I'm torn between chasing after her and giving my father an earful about his jackass comment.

Remembering Holly's advice from last night—to have a serious conversation with my dad—staying to talk wins out. I'll be able to face her better later if I can tell her I did this now.

"Dad," I say through gritted teeth. "We need to talk."

"I'll say." Dad rubs his forehead. "What were you thinking? Sleeping with Holly? She's not the kind of girl you love and leave."

"I'm well aware of that fact, Dad."

My quick agreement seems to take some of the heat out of his irritation. "So, what? Are you two together now?"

"We didn't exactly have a chance to get around and put labels on things." I clench and unclench my hands at my sides. "But I hope there's a future in this. I like her. A lot."

"Well, shit." Dad gives a sheepish grin. "Then I'm happy for you, son. You couldn't find a better girl to spend your life with." His smile slips away, replaced by a frown. "Of course, that'll really complicate things when you're CEO. She'd be your direct report, which—I know, I know— isn't as bad as if she was your secretary. But it'll still raise some eyebrows."

"That's another thing we need to talk about, but first things first." I sigh and motion for him to sit behind his desk. Once he does, I sink into one of the guest chairs across from him. "Dad, I need to tell you I'm sorry."

"What for?"

"For not getting it. When Mom died." My voice shakes a little and I take a second of breathing in deeply to calm myself. "I shouldn't have accused you of not loving her. I shouldn't have accused you of cheating. I know you loved her. You took such good care of her those last months. And I know you and Joyce didn't get together until after. It just..."

"It seemed like I was moving on too fast."

"It did."

"It probably also didn't help that you caught us in a somewhat compromising position in one of the supply closets."

"Yeah, that definitely didn't help." I flinch at the memory of that. "But I should have given you a chance to explain more. I should have listened."

"Well, shit." Dad runs his hand over his hair, which is still as thick as it was when he was my age. I hope I inherited those genes. "If I'm remembering that day correctly, I don't think I gave you much of a chance to ask questions. I didn't do much to answer your questions."

"Maybe—maybe we can agree to leave all of that in the

past." My lips curve up thinking about Holly's new mantra. "We don't even need to worry about the future. Let's just take every day as it comes. It'll give us a chance to get to know each other again. It'll... it'll give me a chance to get to know Joyce and the two of you together."

"I'd like that. You know." He pauses to clear his throat. "You know, me and Joyce. I love her. It doesn't mean I love your mom any less."

I nod because a lump has lodged in my throat.

"Does this mean you're planning on moving back to take your spot at the helm of the company?" Dad asks.

"About that... Another thing we need to discuss."

"Along with your relationship with Holly."

"The two go hand-in-hand from where I'm sitting." I give a light laugh that's more of a sigh of relief. "But do you mind if we work while we talk?"

Dad's brows furrow. "Work?"

I nod, an idea forming in my head that's too good to ignore. "How are you at making paper snowflakes?"

nine

. . .

HOLLY

Tugging my peacoat more tightly around me, I mentally curse myself for picking vanity over comfort as I near the office building.

It's freaking freezing tonight. While my big puffy coat may not have looked as classy with my buffalo print dress, black tights, and spiky red heels, my teeth would definitely be chattering a lot less.

I pull up short when I near the front door to find none other than a certain blonde-haired woman with a bright smile ringing her bell with her bucket.

"You're here!" I exclaim with a mixture of shock, concern, and a small, selfish dash of delight. "You must be freezing."

"Oh, don't you worry, Holly dear." Somehow her smile brightens even more. "I have lots of layers to keep me warm."

"Are you still raising money for the shelter?"

"Of course. Every little bit helps. Now, on to more important things." She gives me a once-over. "You look gorgeous."

"Thanks, I…" My cheeks flush. "I wanted to look good for the Christmas Eve party."

"And may I say mission accomplished. Now, go on." She gives one of her gloved fingers a twirl. "Give yourself a little spin so I can see the full effect."

Shaking my head, but grinning to myself, I oblige, putting my arms in the air like a ballerina as I balance on my heels.

"It's just as I suspected," she says when I come to a stop. "You are positively stunning." Her brow knits together. "Is something wrong?"

At this point, I don't even have to ask how she knows. The woman is either psychic or deeply intuitive.

I take a deep breath, wincing only slightly as the frigid air fills my lungs. "I need a little courage."

"I see. Why don't you tell me what's going on?"

The words spill out of me. I tell her—in PG terms—what happened yesterday, last night, and this morning with Jonas. I tell her about my concerns and fears for my job and heart. I tell her how much I miss my mom and sisters and the holidays we used to share.

Through it all, she listens intently. Nodding her head in encouragement. Crooning in sympathy when my words call for it.

Showing me, by example, what it means to truly and selflessly be there for another person. Even someone who is a virtual stranger.

"So, with all of that, I wanted to look good for the party. Not because I expect it to be my coronation. Ike made it pretty clear who will be the new CEO of Noble Outerwear. And... I can't fault his decision."

I'm also not all dressed up because I think anything more will happen with Jonas. No matter how I might feel about him, there's no way it could work between us. Not if he's about to become my boss.

"I..." I take another deep breath, this time it's not quite so painfully cold as the others. "I wanted to look my best tonight, because... well, because it feels like everything in my life is falling apart." I pause, holding in a sob and giving myself a moment to collect myself.

My friend reaches forward and takes my hand, giving me the silent support I need to continue. "I wanted to stay home. So much. It seemed like it would be easier to curl up in front of the tree, eat sugar cookie dough straight from the bowl, and cry my eyes out while watching an old Christmas movie. Wishing my mom and sisters were there with me. Instead, I put on the new dress I bought just for tonight. I took extra time with my hair and makeup. Because I had the thought that maybe, just maybe, if I look my best tonight, I'll feel my best. Or at least I'll feel better than my worst."

"Well, Holly, I just have to say I'm so impressed by you." She squeezes my hand. "I think you've learned your lesson."

I shake my head in confusion. "What lesson?"

"You've learned to be in the moment. Yes, you're worried about what might happen in the future. Yes, you're struggling with the past that you miss so much. But you came here tonight, determined not to let either of those things keep you from making the best of this moment you have." She reaches out and pats me on the cheek. "That's a lesson some people take their whole lives to learn."

"I... I..." I purse my lips together and cock my head to the side. "I still wish I knew what to do about... everything."

"Don't we all, my dear." She winks. "Don't worry about tomorrow. Enjoy tonight. Allow yourself to feel what you feel. And when you wake up tomorrow, do the same thing."

"I'll try."

"I have no doubt you will." She gives my cheek another pat and my hand another squeeze before reaching to pick up her bell again. "I don't have a crystal ball. I can't see the future. But I have a good feeling about what the future holds for you. If you can just keep yourself centered in the present, everything else—your career, your family, even your love life with a certain strapping young man—will come together."

Another urge to cry rushes over me quickly. Only this time, they aren't tears or sadness. They aren't tears of joy, either. They're the tears of knowing someone—even a woman you've had a handful of interactions with—understands you and knows just what to say to bolster your courage.

"Thank you. I needed to hear that." Lifting my chin, I smile at her confidently. "I think I'm ready to go inside."

"I know you're ready."

"Would you... would you like to come to the party? You'd be very welcome, and we have plenty of food and drinks," I add, anticipating any concerns she might have.

"Thank you for the offer, but I actually have another engagement. I should actually be leaving for it." She gives me another one of her signature smiles. "Remember that old saying: 'Life is a gift, enjoy the present.' I have a hunch your present will be truly remarkable."

I start to move past her, but—on impulse—I turn on my heel and throw my arms around her. Squeezing her tightly.

I lean back. "Thank you for everything." A lump lodges in my throat. Given that she could play a Rose from *The Golden Girls* impersonator for some extra cash on the side, it's tempting to add, 'Thank you for being a friend,' but now isn't a time for jokes. "You've helped me more than I can say. I'll always remember what you've said."

"It was my pleasure."

We give each other parting smiles and I enter the building. Not only do I feel warmer on the outside, but there's a rich heat in my chest. When I reach the bay of elevators, I look over my shoulder to wave at my friend, but she's already gone. She really did have somewhere to be.

I wonder if I'll see her again. Maybe next Christmas? If not… well… I'll take the lesson she gave me to heart and be grateful she was ever in my life. Even if it was only for a short time.

Stepping onto the elevator, I brace myself for whatever awaits me upstairs, determined to keep myself in the moment. No matter what happens.

ten

. . .

HOLLY

The elevator reaches the Noble Outerwear floor and I take a deep breath as the doors open. I can do this. I don't need to worry about what happened earlier today. I don't need to think about what the future holds. I just need to be present.

The doors open, and Linda and Diane practically pounce on me, pulling me out.

"Whoa!" I grip their hands, which have each clasped onto mine, to keep myself upright. "What's going on?"

"You're finally here," Linda says, releasing my hand so she can remove my coat.

Diane is already working on taking off my gloves and sticking them in my purse. "We've been waiting forever."

"I'm only a few minutes late." My eyes widen. "Did something happen with the catering? Did they forget to bring—"

"No, no, no. Everything with the party is fine. In fact,

it's better than fine." A hint of mischief lights Linda's eyes. "We're just dying for you to see how fine it is."

Puzzled, I allow them to hand my things off to the coat check and pull me into the office. I step through the threshold and my breath catches in my throat.

In the hours since I've been gone, the whole place has been transformed. In addition to all of the decorations Jonas and I painstakingly put up before our lock-in, there must be several hundred strings of fairy lights strung and twinkling from the ceiling. Among them, there are hundreds—maybe thousands—of paper snowflakes and streamers.

Buddy the elf may have transformed his family's home into a Christmas wonderland with these decorations in his movie. But a very real—and very busy—elf has been hard at work here.

And I have a sneaky suspicion I know exactly who that elf might be. I just wonder what all this means.

"Where is Jonas... Noble?" I add quickly, hoping not to give anything away by sounding too familiar?

"I believe Baby Noble is waiting outside of your office," Diane says.

Linda smirks. "If I'm not mistaken, there might be a fresh bundle of mistletoe hanging overhead."

So much for not giving anything away. But... who cares? Let the office gossip. I'll worry about that in the future. Right now, all that matters is the right now.

Buzzing with anticipation, I make my way across the office floor. I nod at colleagues and their plus ones along the way. But I don't stop to talk. I have somewhere to be and someone to see.

Out of the corner of my eye, I see Ike Noble dressed as Santa, passing out gifts to the children of our co-workers. The past few days—and particularly this morning—may have complicated things between myself and my mentor. No matter what happens, I will always remember the lessons that he has taught me in my years working for him.

When I round the last row of cubicles, I slow my pace giving my nerves, and my heart, a chance to settle down. Then Jonas—who looks every bit as good in a suit as he does in his flannel and denim, steps into view—and my heart is racing again.

I like him. A lot. I won't say it's love. It's too soon for that.

But if he keeps making my heart pound the way it is right now—if he keeps looking at me with that warm glint in his dark brown eyes—it won't be long before I can put a name to these feelings churning inside of me.

I slow to a stop when I'm a couple of feet from Jonas. I'm tempted to throw myself into his arms. I consider it for a moment, and with a laugh, I do just that.

His arms come around me, the strength in them pulling me close. He presses a kiss to the top of my head, and my heart is pounding once again.

"Well, hello to you," he says, kissing my temple this time. "I'm glad you're happy to see me too. I wasn't sure you would be."

His words, like his touch, flood my soul with joy. I'm glad I gave caution to the wind and gave in to the urge to hug him. It may have been a risk given our past. It may complicate things in the future. But at this moment, there's nowhere else I'd rather be.

"I am." I give him another squeeze before leaning back in his arms so I can see his face. "So glad."

"I missed you." He pulls a face. "Do I lose cool points for admitting that?"

"You earn cool points for saying it." I beam at him. "I like what you've done with the place."

"These old decorations?" He glances around us and lifts his shoulder as if it's no big deal. The slight flush in his cheeks suggest otherwise. "They only took all day to do."

I shake my head, once again admiring the decorations in awe. "I can't believe you made this many in a day."

"Well, I had a little help."

I blink in surprise. "Oh?"

His cheeks turn adorably pink. "I recruited the old man and a few little elves."

Then a grin spreads across his lips. He nods over my shoulder. I turn to see Linda and Diane giggling like little girls instead of grown women.

I give a short laugh. "Some elves. You did all of this for me?"

He nods slowly, his expression sobering. "I told my dad I don't want to be CEO."

I suck in a breath. "What?"

"And I told him he'd be a fool not to hand our family's company over to the person who has lived it all these years and breathed new life into it."

"You—you said that?"

"I did." His lips curve up to the side. "I meant every word. Noble Outerwear wouldn't still be here without you. You're the right person for the job. You're the best person for the job."

My heart fills to the brim. Not because assuming his father takes his advice, I'll fulfill my dream of seeing my nameplate with "CEO" written after it. But because this man has so much unwavering faith and belief in me.

How did that happen so quickly? What does it mean for

our future? Where—No. No, I'm not going to let myself go down either of those paths.

Stay present.

"Thank you." My throat swells. "That hardly seems like enough to say, but… thank you."

"You don't have to thank me. But if you wanted to…" He chuckles, a sound I could really get used to hearing. "I hope you'll consider me when you're hiring a CFO. A company of this size should have one."

From what I know of Jonas and the work he's been doing the past decade, we'd be lucky to have him. With both of us at the helm, nothing could get in our way.

But I can't resist teasing him a little. "So is that how this works? You talk your dad into giving me a job and now you sweet talk me into giving you the one you wanted all along?"

"Pretty much." He laughs again, and I can feel it in my soul. "It might raise some eyebrows—the CEO and the CFO dating and all. But we can put checks and balances into place to protect the company's best interests."

I'm so happy, I'm surprised my heart doesn't burst.

"I think I can agree to those terms."

"Good." He gives me a pointed look. "Now, I don't know if you noticed, but we happen to be standing under some mistletoe."

"Is that what that is?" I glance up and pretend to look confused. "I thought it might be some weeds."

"Trust me, it's mistletoe. I had to call five stores to find it. So." He arches an eyebrow. "What do you say?"

"I'd say you better kiss me right this moment."

"Is that an order from the CEO or my girlfriend?"

My belly flutters. "Can it be from both?"

"I sure hope so."

We're both smiling when our lips meet. We've both been doing that a lot this past day—smiling and kissing. Past Me would've been worried about what everyone here at the party must think. Past Me would worry about what this means for Future Me at work and in life.

As for Present Me? She's just happy to be standing under a mistletoe in an office decorated like a winter wonderland, kissing a man who makes life anything but boring.

There really is something to learning to live in the present. It's turning out to be the best gift ever.

epilogue

. . .

One year later...

JONAS

I barely get into position before Holly waltzes into her office.

"Okay, the decorations are done. The caterer will be here in half an hour. And your dad and Joyce are getting into their Santa and Mrs. Claus costumes as we speak," she reads off from the checklist she has on her phone. "That means we have about twenty minutes to finish getting ready and..."

She tears her gaze from the phone and gasps.

I can't help but grin at the fact it took her almost two full minutes to notice the way I've transformed her office into the winter wonderland she loves so much from *Elf*.

"What..." Then she turns to me and sucks in a breath again.

I'm kneeling on the floor just inside the door of her office.

"A year and two days ago, I saw you for the first time," I

say, taking care with each word. "You took my breath away. At first, I thought it was because you knocked the door handle into my dick."

She gives a short laugh at that, but her eyes are already filling with tears.

My own voice is thick with emotion. "You were so striking. Seeing you was like being struck by lightning. It didn't take me long to realize what exactly that meant. It didn't take me long to realize it was me, falling completely in love with you."

I take a moment to swallow and reach for her hand. She shakily slips it into mine. "I want to spend my life loving you. I want to make a life with you. A family. I want us to make so many Christmas memories and cherish every day in between."

I beam up at her. "Holly Carol, will you be my wife?"

"Yes." She bobs her head up and down. "Will you be my husband?"

"Absolutely."

I slide a ring onto her finger and she throws herself into my arms. I pull her close, kissing her with all of the love in my heart.

There's a cheer in the background and we break apart. Outside of the office, a small crowd has gathered. My dad and my stepmom. Her sisters, Ivy and Merry, and their other halves.

"I hope you don't mind." I brush my lips over hers again. "I know it's the Christmas Eve party, but I thought we might make it a bit of an engagement celebration too."

"I think it's a great idea." She grins and presses her lips to mine. "Just so long as you don't use company funds. As the CEO, it's important for me to keep track of these things. And as CFO, you should—"

I silence her, deepening the kiss, forgetting that we have an audience. It's the first kiss of our promise to each other. A promise for hundreds and thousands of days of finding joy together.

Easing up on the kiss, my lips curve into a matching grin against hers. Ending it so we can both breathe, I beam at her. All of the love in my heart filled to the brim.

I wonder if I can talk her into sneaking back into her office later after we greet our employees. We can pretend that the doorknob is broken. I'm sure we'll find a way to pass the time.

I stand up and offer her a hand, helping her smooth out her dress. I start to speak but frown as I see another person standing behind our families, who are all excitedly chatting.

It's a woman who looks familiar. I don't know that I've met her, but there's… something about her.

"Holly?"

She strokes my cheek and I lean into her touch. "Yes, my love?"

"I know this might sound crazy. But… Is it just me, or does the woman standing over there look just like Rose from *The Golden Girls*?"

❆

Read more from Kate Tilney!
Click here to subscribe to her newsletter and get a free read.

merry and the ghost of christmas future

Lana Dash

one

. . .

MERRY

As a kid, I loved listening for my mother at the stroke of
midnight on November 1st. She'd creep into the attic and
pull out all of the Christmas decorations to get set up
overnight. No one loved the holidays as much as she did,
and if you doubt her dedication to the holiday, I give you
the names she gave her three daughters—Ivy, Holly, and
Merry.

I'm Merry. But I'm not feeling very merry right now.

The twinkle lights I never took down from last year still
hang around my studio apartment, sparkling like the night
sky outside. The crooning voice of Dean Martin almost
nearly drowns out the sounds of life in the streets of Denver
down below as he sings about having a Blue Christmas.

I hear ya, Deano.

My merriment for the holiday season has lost its spark
this year, and there is nothing I or anyone can do to bring it

back. Because this will be the first year my sisters and I will be without our mother since she passed suddenly over the summer.

As the youngest of the three Carol triplets, I'd always tease my sisters that I was our mother's favorite child. And whenever I'd ask Mom to back me up, she'd just smile and say, "You, my sweet Merry, are my favorite *youngest* daughter." Much to my disappointment and the amusement of Ivy and Holly.

The ornament I haven't stopped staring at since I opened my Christmas box says nearly that—Favorite Youngest Child. We each got one indicating our placement at birth last Christmas.

Ivy is the oldest, with the work ethic and responsibility that so many firstborns seem to possess. As for Holly, she's the Jan Brady of our little trio. That is to say that she's the middle child. And she's got to contend with Ivy's colossal shadow and my loud mouth, so her outgoing personality and stubborn streak keeps her from being forgotten. But never one to be outdone by my sisters, I quickly learned to embrace my flare for the dramatics and laissez-faire attitude. To me, the future can't be planned (don't tell Ivy) or perfect (don't tell Holly). Instead, it's limitless with all its possibilities, so I like to take each day as it comes.

The song ends, and Dean starts singing about marshmallows in the winter, but I'm not in the mood to hear anything happy.

"Allegra, next song," I yell to the speaker sitting on the bookshelf.

"Okay, turning up song."

"What?" I lift my head off the couch as Dean sings louder from the speaker. "I didn't say to turn up the song!"

"Okay, turning up song."

"No!" I yell, but the happy near-deafening notes swallow up my voice.

At that moment, the screen on my phone lights up with a smiling picture of my best friend, Amy, and me. We took it while we were backpacking through Europe after high school graduation and stopped in Prague.

"Hang on, Ames!" I yell by way of greeting.

She says something, but I can't hear anything she is saying. I roll off the couch to stand up, but my foot catches on the Christmas box sitting on the ground near the coffee table. I spin around to try and avoid falling over but knock right into the undecorated Fraser Fir I lugged up five flights to get here. Neither one of us stands a chance of staying upright, and we both fall, with me taking the brunt of the impact.

"Son of a nutcracker!" I grunt under its weight.

Amy yells into the phone, asking if I'm okay. It just barely cuts through the sound of the blaring music. I reach for the phone a few feet away, but I'm trapped.

"Hang on, Ames!" I yell again as I stretch for the one thing I *can* get my hands on—the cord of the Allegra.

Yanking hard on the cord, I pull it free from the wall, ending the barrage of holiday notes.

"Are you dead?" Amy yells again, but I can hear her crystal clear now.

I shimmy a few inches until my fingertips brush across the phone's edges, and I slide it over to me.

"Okay," I say, holding it up to my ear. "I'm here."

"What the hell just happened?" she asks.

I look down at the wreckage of the fallen fir lying on top of me. "You'd never believe it even if I told you."

Amy chuckles on the other end. "Coming from you, I've learned to believe the crazy things that come from your mouth. Everyone does."

She's not wrong.

"What's going on?" I ask, scooting myself out, inch by inch.

"I need you to come to Vermont."

"I am," I tell her. "I've already got my ticket for the new year. Don't worry. I will be at your wedding, standing next to you on the second Saturday in January."

Amy doesn't need to know that Ivy was the one who reminded me for the umpteenth time yesterday to get my ass into gear and buy my ticket, or else I would be driving cross country to watch my best friend get married.

"No, that was the plan, but something's happened."

I don't miss the note of panic in her voice when she says this. "What's wrong?"

"Nathan's grandmother hasn't been doing so well, and his parents asked if we'd be willing to move up the wedding, you know, just in case—" she fades off, explaining without fully explaining. She's worried about saying the words in front of me because of my mom.

"I totally get it," I assure her. "When do you need me? I will find a ticket. And if I can't get a ticket, I'll borrow Holly's car and drive there for you. Just name the date. I will be there."

Amy lets out a sigh of relief that she'd been holding. "Christmas day."

Uh oh. My sisters are not going to like this.

"Umm, okay. I know I said to name the date, but—"

"I know, Mere. I'm sorry. This whole wedding is spinning wildly out of control. It's like it's not even about us anymore. I didn't get to pick the venue. I was told that I'd be wearing his mother's dress like it was a done deal. And now this." Almost as soon as the words come out of her mouth, she groans like she suddenly remembers why the date needs to be changed. "Now I sound like such a bridezilla."

"You are not a bridezilla. Far from it. If anything, I think you've taken all this in stride." It's clear that Amy needs someone there by her side to make sure that she's okay. "I'll be there. I don't know what I'm going to say to Ivy or Holly, but I'll think of something."

"I don't know what I'd do without you," Amy says, sounding so relieved. "Which is why this next part will make you really not like me."

"Not possible." I smile.

"Katherine's bringing a date," she blurts out.

"Nathan's sister? I'm pretty sure I was expecting to see your fiancé's sister at the wedding."

"Yeah, but there's something you need to know about who she is bringing."

I laugh. "As long as you tell me it isn't Chad, I can handle whoever he is."

The silence on the other end makes my heart sink like a rock into my stomach. This can't be happening.

"Amy."

Silence.

"Amy!"

"I'm sorry!" she finally says. "I didn't know about it until this morning, and I've been working up the courage to tell you all day."

Katherine's schoolgirl crush on my ex-boyfriend Chad was a point of contention between us at the end of our relationship. It wasn't the only issue we had, but it certainly was a big one. He claimed that she was just friendly, but I thought the constant flirting and touching him was inappropriate. Of course, I knew it was the right call at the time, but it sucks to find out just how right I was with my suspicions.

"Mere, what are you thinking?"

"I'm thinking I need a date for your wedding."

two

. . .

OSCAR

"What do you mean they are going forward with the list?" I ask angrily into my phone.

The substitute driver that the car service sent over, since Thomas is back in Dublin with his family for the holidays, glances into the rearview mirror and we lock eyes. He makes the tiniest sound like a nervous squeak before his eyes dart back to the road.

I like that I have that effect on people. All it takes is one look, and they don't know what to do or where to look. They get so flustered that I quickly hold all the power in this equation. It's helped me immensely in the corporate world. I've built my company up from nothing and made myself one of the wealthiest people in the country.

"I did everything I could to try and get you off the list," my publicist, Anna, says calmly into my ear. "But after you sold your company and joined the billionaire boys club, did you really think they were going to leave you off the Most Eligible Bachelors under Forty list?"

"I thought that's what I was paying you for," I growl.

"Down, boy," Anna chuckles. "I did manage to get you off the cover. At least I spared the world from having to see that surly face glaring up at them from the magazine racks while they stand in line at the grocery store."

Anna is one of the few people that still talks to me this way. As much as I enjoy giving off that grumpy demeanor to most of the people I come across, I only let the people I really care about see that there is a softer side of me.

"I should fire you."

"Ha!" She laughs. "Good luck finding someone new that could do what I do."

"You know I hate fake people buzzing around me, looking for some handout."

"We both know that you have no problem opening that rather large wallet of yours to help anyone in need, not that you'd let me share that with the world."

"I don't do it for the recognition."

"I know, I know." She sighs. "Your lack of interest in sharing this knowledge with the world is probably the only reason the magazine was okay with replacing you on the cover with Matteo Baez."

"I don't know who that is."

"The baseball player."

I shake my head. "Doesn't ring any bells."

"You are unbelievable. Maybe your complete lack of knowledge when it comes to pop culture is the reason you haven't found some lucky girl to settle down with."

The car starts to slow down near the front of my private hanger and I look up to see a woman I don't know standing at the foot of my jet's steps, bouncing on her toes, like a kid who is about to meet Santa Claus. She's wearing a trapper hat with flaps hanging down on each side of her head. This must be Amy's maid of honor I'm taking with me to Vermont.

"I'm never going to settle down," I say.

"Never say never," Anna sing-songs before hanging up the phone.

"We're here, sir," the driver says, pulling to a stop. His eyes are cast down like he's still afraid to look at me.

A pang of guilt hits me when I think of someone treating Thomas this way. I reach into my front pocket and pull out my wallet. I pull a few crisp hundred-dollar bills out and lean forward in my seat.

"Merry Christmas," I say, reaching over the seat and handing him the folded cash.

His eyes light up when he turns to see what I'm offering him. "Thank you, sir."

"Don't mention it," I tell him, meaning it literally, and opening my door for myself to step out of the town car.

I'm not sure if it's because I've become accustomed to a certain level of recognition since I sold my company or what, but when the woman's eyes meet mine, there is no recognition. It's an odd feeling, almost a relief, when she doesn't change her demeanor as I approach. But the relief is fleeting when she turns back to the pilot and continues to talk animatedly to him like I don't exist. A surge of possessiveness hits me from out of nowhere when I realize I don't want to share her hazel-eyed attention with anyone, especially with this pretty boy pilot.

"I'd say a little over five hours," the pilot responds to her question about how long the flight will be.

I'm about to tell him that I'm ready to go when she turns

to me and asks, "Can you believe Nathan's family sent this for us to fly to the wedding?"

I'm confused for a moment, but before I can respond, she continues. "I mean, I figured he was from old crusty New England money with a name like Winthrop-Bower, but this is nice."

Pretty Boy Pilot starts to open his mouth to clear up her misunderstanding by explaining that this is in fact my plane, but I give him the smallest of headshakes to stop him.

"Yes," I agree with her. "Very generous."

"I'm Mere, by the way." She holds out her hand to me.

I take it in mine. "Oscar."

"I hope you aren't anything like the green fella you share your name with," she chuckles to herself.

I don't miss the side-eyed smirk that Pretty Boy Pilot shares with his co-pilot. But when they catch my narrow-eyed gaze on them, they both look down at their feet nervously.

"I think we should get going," I say and gesture for her to go up the steps first.

The excitement that lights up her beautiful face awakens something in me that I haven't felt in a long time, but I push it away. I'm not looking for any romantic entanglements right now. I don't need the complications and hassle that they always seem to bring into my life.

"Are you freaking kidding me?" Mere shouts when she gets a look at the inside of the plane.

I wait patiently, standing behind her as she takes in the luxury cabin. After traveling this way for the last few years, I don't see what she is seeing at this moment. For a while now, I've become so desensitized by all that I have. It's refreshing to be around someone who doesn't have expectations about who I am because of my name or my money.

Mere turns around and smacks me in the arm lightly. "Can you believe this?"

"It really is something." I nod and follow her over to the two cushioned chairs that face one another.

"My sisters are never going to believe this," she says, holding up her phone and taking a selfie.

As I sit down my phone pings an alert from inside my front pocket. I pull it out and see a text message from Anna with only one word, *"shit."* There's a link, and I press it, knowing already what I'm going to see. Just as she predicted but failed to stop, my unsmiling face is staring out from the cover.

three

. . .

MERRY

There's something familiar about Oscar that I just can't put my finger on. I don't know if it's because every guy in a suit looks the same to me or what, but it's clear from his grim expression that he isn't happy about whatever it is he sees on his phone. I can practically see the steam coming out of his ears as he drops his phone down on the table between us.

"Everything okay?" I ask.

He looks up at me with a look that I'm sure would have anyone shaking in their snow boots, but for some reason, he reminds me of an angry bear that just needs a hug.

"Nothing you need to worry about."

I shrug and glance out the small window next to me and watch as the Denver winter backdrop starts to move. This flight is a once-in-a-lifetime experience, and I'm not going to let Oscar, the grouch across from me, ruin any of it.

We are in the air in no time, and the flight attendant

comes over to us and offers us each an espresso and a chocolate chip cookie. Oscar takes a sip of his coffee and completely ignores his cookie.

"Are you going to eat that?" I ask, around the cookie that I practically jammed into my mouth. It was too warm and gooey not to eat it all at once.

Oscar pushes his plate a few inches toward me and watches with interest as I waste no time eating his.

"I skipped breakfast," I say, but that's a lie. This is a full-on second breakfast for me. And if he had more, I would have eaten those. "What?"

"You've got," he points to his face to gesture that I have something on mine.

I use the back of my hand to wipe at the corner of my mouth. "Did I get it?"

"No." He shakes his head and reaches over to me, and uses his thumb to rub across the bottom part of my lip. "Got it."

I watch as he licks the melted chocolate off his thumb like it's the most natural thing to happen between two people who have just met. Never mind the fact that my imagination explodes with so many scenarios in my mind at what he can do with that tongue. I need to get my head back on track.

"We have some hours to kill before we get there." I pull off my hat and run my fingers through my hair. "Come on, lay it on me. What's bothering you?"

"I don't think so."

"Maybe we could be of use to one another."

Oscar's left eyebrow lifts suggestively at me. "How so?"

"Not that way, you perv," I roll my eyes, but I don't miss the flutter of something in my stomach when the corner of his mouth ticks up slightly.

"You sure?" He smirks. "I'm pretty sure there's a bedroom in the back."

I glance over my shoulder to the closed door behind me and then back at him.

As tempting as it might be to shock my sisters with a story about having sex in a private plane with a stranger, I'm not looking for any complications on this trip. My life is already complicated enough since Holly is upset that I won't be home for Christmas since I'm going to Amy's wedding. Not that she'd ever admit it out loud to Ivy or me for not staying in Denver. But there's also the fact that I'm about to run into my ex at a wedding with his new girl-friend while I'm flying solo.

"There's something else I need from you," I say.

Oscar plays the strong silent type well and continues to stare at me without saying a word.

"I need a date," I continue. There's no reason to beat around the bush with this guy. "My ex is on the other end of this flight, and I need someone by my side that is going to make him think twice about letting me go."

Oscar's eyes narrow on me, and the silence that settles between us is nearly unbearable. His dark eyes are unread-able, and the closely shaven beard he's got puts Chad's patchy facial hair to shame.

"And you think that I'm that man?" he finally asks.

I'm not one to fan the flame of some hot guy's ego, but I'm wondering if Oscar really doesn't know how good looking he is. "Do I need to hold a mirror up for you to see what the world sees?"

The smirk returns, and instead of flutters in my belly, the flutters have relocated to a lower place on my body. This should be a warning that what I'm proposing to him is incredibly dangerous, but I'm a desperate woman. I need a point in the win column for once, and if that win comes from a loss for Chad, then I will do anything to make it happen.

"If we do this, we're going to do it right," he says.

"What do you mean?"

"No one can know the truth,"

"I'm mean, I have to tell Amy," I start to say, but his head shake stops me.

"No one can know."

The curiosity of why this stranger is actually playing along in my crazy scheme is killing me, but I don't want him to change his mind. He obviously has his reasons, and I have mine. I'm just more vocal about it than him.

"That means we have to share a room," I say. It's not a question but a statement.

"Is that a problem for you?" he asks.

"No." I shake my head. "What are the terms of PDA?"

"Naturally, I'll let you take the lead on what you feel comfortable with."

"And what do you feel comfortable with?"

Oscar smiles and leans on the table between us. "I wouldn't worry about me."

Every single cell in my body is screaming at me to abort this crazy plan. How am I going to not get lost in those dark eyes when he keeps looking at me like that? But do I listen? Nope.

"Are you in love with me?" I ask.

This question actually takes him by surprise, and he sits back in his seat. "No."

"Good," I nod and hold out my hand to lock down this business arrangement. "Let's keep it that way, and we won't have a problem."

four

. . .

OSCAR

By the time the plane lands, we are shuttled into the town car waiting for us in the hangar. Our plan for a fake relationship at this wedding is in full swing, and we are both ready to play our parts.

Merry's laid out her reason for wanting to enter into this fake relationship with me, but I haven't told her my reasons. Not that she asked, but I wouldn't have told her either way. I can't take the chance that she will turn into all the other women around me when they find out who I am and what I'm worth. If having her on my arm will keep away any single women at this wedding from trying to hit on me, then all this nonsense will be worth it—especially dealing with Katherine.

Nathan's younger sister has made it very clear from nearly the moment we met that she was interested in something more between us. But she is nothing more to me than my best friend's younger sister. I've endured multiple attempts by her to persuade me otherwise, but I've never changed my mind, and I won't start this weekend.

"This is where Amy and Nathan are getting married?" Merry asks, staring out the window as we pull to a stop in front of the Black Forrest Lodge.

It's a four-story Tudor-style ski lodge with greenery hanging on each balcony with red ribbons attached and twinkle lights hanging in all the surrounding pine trees.

"Nathan's family owns this place and quite a few more up and down the east coast," I explain.

"Is that how you know him?" she glances over her shoulder at me.

"No, we went to boarding school together." I don't explain that I was the son of the groundskeeper while it was actually Nathan who was attending the school.

"Hmm," Merry says and turns back to the window.

I want to know what she means by that noise, but there's no time to ask her. One of the valets standing at the podium runs over to the town car and opens her door.

"Welcome to the Black Forrest Lodge," he says, offering her his hand with an overly friendly smile that disappears the moment he notices me.

Merry gets out, and I follow after her. Considering we are trying to play this new pretend role of boyfriend and girlfriend with one another, it should be awkward. But without thinking twice, we both reach for one another like it's the most natural thing in the world. Her soft hand fits in mine like a glove.

"Ready to do this?" She asks.

I glance over at her and lean close. "It's already begun."

A squeal behind us makes us both turn to see Katherine pushing out the Lodge doors and running towards me.

"Nathan said you were coming, but I told him I'd

believe it when I see it," she says, throwing her arms around my neck.

Merry tries to pull her hand from mine in an attempt to allow me to give Katherine a proper hug, but I don't let go of her. The number one reason I'm playing pretend this weekend is right in front of me, and I don't want her to think anything has changed since the last time she threw herself at me, and I turned her down.

MERRY

I'm not prepared for the surge of jealousy that strikes me when I watch as Katherine tries to practically climb Oscar like he's a mountain, not a man. I thought I was past most of my ill feelings for her at this point, but I think I was being too optimistic. Why else would I want to grab Katherine by the back of her head and yank her off him?

"I missed seeing you at the vineyard over Thanksgiving," Katherine says in that whiney flirty way some women think is charming. "It's not the same when you aren't there."

"He was busy with me." The words are out of my mouth before I even realize I've said them.

Both Katherine and Oscar swing their gazes over at me with two very different expressions on their faces. Oscar looks surprisingly amused by my admission, while Katherine's nose crinkles up like she's just smelled something rotten.

"Really?" She looks from me to Oscar. The once genuine smile on her face a moment ago is replaced with one that is completely forced. Her eyelids blink rapidly like she's inwardly hoping that she's dreaming and that what I've just said is entirely untrue. If only she knew. "When did this happen?"

"Well," Oscar says, wrapping his arm over my shoulder and pulling me into his side. "It happened kind of suddenly."

The meltdown brewing behind Katherine's calm demeanor is interrupted by her brother and my best friend walking out of the lodge to greet us. Amy and Nathan look excited to see us, but I don't miss the quizzical glance shared between them when they see how Oscar is holding onto me.

"What's going on?" Amy mouths to me when no one is looking.

There's no way I can answer her truthfully without breaking one of the rules Oscar and I agreed to, so I just shrug my shoulders and smile. If I play it off like it's no big deal, Amy might chalk this up to just another crazy antic from her best friend. To be honest, this doesn't even make the top-ten crazy things I've done, and Amy was a witness to most of it. I'm not worried.

A cold blast of winter wind kicks up, and we all move into the lobby of the lodge with a group of other people standing around as if they've only just arrived as well.

I can't stop myself from looking around for Chad. It's not like I want to see him. It's more like I'd like a moment to mentally prepare myself for the first run we will have since our break up before I can put on my fake smile for everyone.

Raised voices from the front desk draw our small group's attention. And that's when I see my ex standing at the counter arguing with someone from management in the lodge.

"Is that him?" Oscar whispers to me. "You're ex."

"How'd you guess?"

"Just a feeling."

I turn to ask him what that means when I notice a unique sight heading our way.

An older woman, who looks well into her eighties, is wearing a bright green jogging suit and powerwalking through the Lodge lobby. She can't be more than a breath above five feet, and her silvery-white hair is curled and sprayed so much that it doesn't move on top of her head.

I stare awestruck at her. She's what I dream of being like when I'm her age, looking hot and not giving a shit about what anyone thinks of her.

"I want to be her someday," I whisper to Oscar.

He glances distractedly at me from Nathan and Amy as they present the wedding plans for the next couple of days.

"Who?" he asks.

I go to point out the woman to him, but she's already gone. "Never mind."

"We know that you all gave up a lot to be here," Nathan says. "Amy and I want you to know how much we couldn't have imagined celebrating our wedding without any of you."

Katherine drags Chad over to the group and hangs on his arm like he's singlehandedly the only reason she is currently standing upright.

Memories of our time together flash in my mind like it's being projected on a screen in front of me. We were happy for the most part, at least, I thought we were. But despite my efforts to try and be the person that Chad wanted me to be—more serious, someone who could plan things further in the future than seventy-two hours—the real me slipped through.

As much as I'd love to blame Katherine entirely for the

break up of our relationship, she was just the final straw that broke the camel's back. Chad wanted me to be Miss Right, but I could only be Miss Right Now. I don't think I'll ever meet someone that I could see myself planning a future with.

Despite my efforts to pretend like I don't see him, Chad tries to make eye contact with me. It's like my non-reaction to seeing him can only be explained in his head by the fact that I must not have noticed him standing there and not that I'm over us.

This sudden understanding of what I feel, or instead what I don't feel for him, takes a weight off my shoulders that I didn't know I was carrying around. This realization has me thinking about Oscar. This whole ruse was built around the fact that I cared what Chad thought about me. But if that isn't a factor I need to worry about, I don't really need a fake boyfriend.

Oscar must feel my stare because he looks over at me and gives me a reassuring half-smile that makes the blood in my veins heat up. My brain is yelling at me to tell him the truth, but other parts of my body are keeping my lips locked up tight.

five

. . .

OSCAR

"Did I miss something since the last time we spoke?" Nathan asks me. "I mean, according to a certain magazine, that shall not be named. You are a bachelor. The most eligible one at that."

He's fishing for some explanation about Merry and me. There's no doubt in my mind that Merry is getting the same line of questioning from Amy. She's sitting with the other two bridesmaids, and she looks like she doesn't want to be here anymore than I do.

It's been a long day of traveling, and the best man and maid of honor can't skip the evening Welcome Cocktails event to kick off this wedding weekend. But a part of me wishes I should have taken Merry up on her offer to order room service and watch Christmas movies in the room. But then again, if we didn't come out tonight, I'd have missed seeing her wear the Christmas cat dress she's got on now. The memory from earlier plays back in my mind.

"Alright, meow," Merry peeks her head out of the bath-room door. "Are you ready?"

I look up from my phone. "Just waiting on you."

I've been dressed and ready to head down to the evening event for twenty minutes, but Merry has been taking her time getting ready.

"You can't rush purr-fection."

"At this point, I'd take mediocre if it gets us out the door quicker."

"Aww, look at us. Are we having our first lover's quarrel?" She smiles like this is a moment she doesn't want to miss.

"Can we go?"

"Come on, grumpy. I'm trying to build up the excitement for my dress reveal."

"Does it involve felines?"

Her smile falters, and she steps out of the bathroom. "How did you know?"

"Your use of cat puns helped me crack the code."

"Well?" she asks, spinning around in place so I can see her dress in all its glory. "What do you think?"

The top half of the dress is tight and black with a matching ribbon tied around the waist, but the bottom half is green and printed with cats wearing Santa hats. This dress is sure to set her apart from all the other guests tonight, but I'm starting to see more and more that's just who Merry is. It's best just to lean in and embrace it.

"It's paw-fect," I say.

Her face lights up at my attempt at a cat pun for her. "If you were my real boyfriend, I'd kiss you right on the mouth for that."

"Hello?" Nathan holds his hand in front of my face. "Are you even listening to me?"

I'm snapped out of the memory and find myself face to face with my best friend.

"What did you say?" I ask.

Nathan smiles and shakes his head. "I was asking you how it is that you and Mere happened, but from the way you were just looking at her, I think I already got my answer."

I'm about to open my mouth and explain that I'm not looking at her in any certain way, but just as quickly, I remember that I need to play this role. I've already seen a few women circling us like sharks as we stand here as if they smell my bachelorhood like chum in the water.

"What can I say?" I shrug. "When you know it's right, why hold back?"

Nathan studies me like he's not sure if he should believe what I'm saying or not, but thankfully we get interrupted when some other guests walk up and start talking with him.

"So, you're the new guy?" A voice asks behind me.

I turn and see Merry's ex swaying slightly as he stands with a drink in his hand. The angry look he's shooting my way looks far less intimidating in his inebriated state.

"I don't think it's any of your concern who I am," I tell him.

He takes an unsteady step toward me, but I don't move. This guy is the least of my concerns, but if he thinks I'm going to let him mess around with Merry's head, he's got another thing coming.

"She's nothing but a good fuck," he practically spits out. "There's no long-term relationship with someone like her."

My body moves quicker than my brain, and I grab him by the lapels of his jacket, lifting him onto his toes.

"I don't ever want to hear you talking about her like that ever again," I say in a harsh whisper. "You got that?"

Nathan appears next to me and pushes his way between us. I let go of this jackass's lapels and step back. Turning around, I find all eyes in the room looking in my direction. I'm not sure what came over me. I usually can keep my poker face in place when I'm dealing with someone trying to get a reaction out of me. But there was something about the way that he spoke about Merry that had me wanting to punch his lights out.

MERRY

I can barely keep my eyes open. There's something about traveling in any direction outside of my time zone that messes with my internal clock, and the heavy-handed pour of alcohol in this cocktail is not helping me to keep my eyes open either. I've played my part of maid of honor for the evening, but I'm ready to call it a night.

"You need to keep those eyes open, dear," a sweet elderly voice says next to me, making me jump.

I look to my right and find the older woman I saw earlier in the lobby sitting next to me. She's changed out of her bright green tracksuit and replaced it with a black one that's bejeweled around the cuffs and collar.

"You don't want to miss what's right in front of you," she continues.

I turn to follow her gaze and see a tipsy Chad walking in the direction of where Oscar is standing with Nathan.

"This can't be good," I mumble, but the woman hears me and chuckles.

"It's tough when the past and the present collide," she

continues and takes a bite of the frosted sugar cookie shaped like a Christmas tree.

This afternoon I thought she was just another guest at the lodge, but seeing as she's here at the welcome event, I'm starting to wonder if this is Nathan's grandmother. She doesn't look sick like Amy had said on the phone. I mean, hell, she was powerwalking the last time I saw her.

It's only at this moment that I realize what she's said to me.

"How did you—" I start to ask but stop when Oscar's angry voice carries across the room to us.

"You got that?" He yells.

I push up from my seat. Everyone at the party has stopped what they are doing to watch the spectacle unfold. Oscar turns around, his eyes wide and searching until they land on me.

"I've got to go," I turn to say to the woman, but she's no longer sitting next to me. The only sign that I didn't make her up was sitting in the form of a half-eaten frosted sugar cookie on the table.

I don't have time to try and figure out if my jetlag is making me see things or not. Instead, I walk around the table and over to Oscar, looping my arm in his.

"Let's go."

He doesn't argue and leads us both out of the banquet room. It isn't until we reach the elevator in the lobby that I glance back over my shoulder. A part of me is worried that Chad will follow, but from what I can see, Katherine is chewing him out.

"That was amazing," I whisper, but it's unnecessary since no one is around to hear us.

"You aren't mad?" he asks.

"Mad?" I scoff. "I wouldn't have cared if you hit him, but that might have ruined the night for Amy and Nathan."

"You continue to surprise me, Merry," Oscar says. "Every time I think you're going to zig, you zag."

"I'm going to take that as a compliment—I think."

Oscar's eyes twinkle with amusement. "You should."

The elevator doors open, and he gestures for me to go in first. His hand rests on my lower back as he leads me in. My body heats up again from his touch. We don't have an audience at the moment, so I'm not sure why he's still playing the boyfriend role, but I'm not in any hurry to stop him.

"If you really want this to be believable," I say to him as the doors close. "You really should be calling me Mere."

six

. . .

OSCAR

The following morning, I wake up to the sounds of Merry's, I mean, Mere's, snoring. She's asleep in the bed while I'm on the sofa, with my tall frame hanging off both ends. My chivalrous nature is the reason my back is going to be killing me all day. Too often, I forget that I'm not that young kid in college who could sleep anywhere and run a marathon the next day if I wanted to.

I sit up and rub my hands over my face. Nothing short of a triple espresso will pull me out of this sleepy morning haze. I'm usually a morning person, but I had a lot on my mind last night.

As much as he deserved it—and much more—Mere's ex really struck a nerve in me that I wasn't expecting. I'd never let someone talk about a woman like that in front of me, but it was different when I heard him talking about her. The possessiveness, the urge to protect her, came over me, and I nearly laid him out in front of all the other guests. It doesn't help that Katherine's attention hasn't been deterred even though she has her own date, and I'm in a relationship with Mere—at least as far as she knows.

Before we fell asleep last night, Mere explained her history with Katherine and how she was a factor in their breakup. Based on Katherine's history of self-serving behavior, I'm not surprised that she'd pull a stunt like this. Her plan was to kill two birds with one stone—hurt Mere and try to make me jealous.

It didn't work with me, but I can't help but wonder if Katherine's shot across the bow wasn't more of a direct hit for Mere. Then again, maybe I don't want to know. I'm not sure the feelings that are growing inside me are still the platonic fake relationship ones I keep telling myself that they are.

There's a soft knock at the door, but the noise doesn't do much to the logs that Mere is sawing in her sleep.

I walk over to the door to answer it. Without thinking, I swing it open, forgetting for a moment that certain people here can't know that I slept on the couch last night. Katherine's perfectly painted face lights up when she sees it's me.

"Oh good," Katherine sighs. "I didn't want Merry answering."

I swing the door back towards me so that my body blocks any view of the room behind me.

"What are you doing here?" I whisper.

"I needed to talk to you."

"Now isn't a good time."

Katherine looks me up and down, her eyes lingering just a bit on my bare chest and abs. I'm not one to shy away from showing off the body I've worked so hard to build, but she isn't the one I want looking at me this way. It's only when Mere pops into my mind that I realize the snoring from earlier has stopped.

"I'm really sorry that Chad came after you like that last night." She reaches out for me, but I pull back so her hand drops between us. "He can be so protective of me. He thinks you are here to win me over."

"Gross," I hear Mere say somewhere in the room behind me, but it's so soft that I'm pretty sure Katherine doesn't hear her.

"I'm only here for the wedding, Katherine. Nothing more."

Not taking no for an answer, she takes a step toward me. But Mere's voice stops her in her tracks.

"Babe?" Mere calls out. "Who is it?"

I glance over my shoulder and see that all signs that I slept on the couch last night are gone—replaced with Mere, wearing only my t-shirt with her bare legs propped up on the edge of the coffee table.

"If it's room service," she continues. "I hope they brought more whipped cream."

The suggestive tone in her voice and the sight of her bare legs are like a shot of adrenaline to my bloodstream, and my dick twitches to attention. I release the door, allowing it to drift open so Katherine can see her too.

"It's not room service," I say.

"Shame." Mere smiles sweetly, but I see the vindication flash in her expression when she and Katherine lock eyes. "I'm so hungry."

Fuck.

Katherine growls in frustration and turns on her heels to leave.

"Wait, don't go," Mere whispers purposefully so Katherine can't hear her.

I can't hold back the bark of laughter that comes out of me. "I don't think she heard you, babe."

MERRY

Why does it feel so right to hear Oscar call me babe? Not to mention the jealousy I felt when I woke up and heard Katherine talking with him at the door. For a moment, I wondered if what I felt was residual anger over what happened with Chad, but the thought of her trying to get close to Oscar lit a fire in me that I'd never felt before.

I was up and out of bed, grabbing all the bedding off the couch and tossing it behind the wall that partially divides the bed and the living area of the suite. Just as I was about to announce my presence, I noticed Oscar's shirt folded on the coffee table. I yanked off my shirt and pulled his on. The woodsy scent of his body wash made my lady bits tingle with excitement. His scent is my new favorite smell, and I hope it lingers on my skin for the rest of the day.

After Katherine storms off, Oscar closes the door behind her with a devilish smile on his face.

"You are incredible," he says, walking over and sitting down next to me.

"Is there something I need to know about you two?" I ask. The words slip out of my mouth before I can turn on my internal filter. I don't have any right to ask him to explain himself to me, but that doesn't mean I don't want to know.

"Are you jealous?" he asks, looking amused and resting his arm on the back of the couch behind me.

"Please," I scoff, but I'm desperately trying to sound

nonchalant. "I'm just trying to understand. She's a beautiful blonde bombshell, and every guy that looks at her falls in love."

"I didn't." His response is so quick and without hesitation that there's no doubt in my mind that he is telling me the truth.

My heart starts to thump in my chest much faster than before, and I have to remind myself to breathe. Oscar's gaze darkens as it dips down to my lips. The lines that we laid about this fake relationship are starting to blur, and I want more than anything to kiss him.

"You don't like blondes?" I whisper.

He shakes his head, and his fingers start to play with the ends of my dark chestnut hair. "I've always been partial to brunettes."

My body is like a teapot on the stove, slowly heating up until I reach my boiling point and I can't hold it in. I lean forward and press my lips against his. He doesn't hesitate, cupping the back of my head with one hand and wrapping his arm around me with the other. I'm pulled onto his lap, straddling his firm thighs and thick cock, our kiss never breaking.

"Mmm," he releases a groan deep in his chest as I press my hips down against him.

Fuck, this feels amazing.

I move my hips in a circle, allowing the friction out our bodies to begin the slow burn of pleasure to build up between us. Oscar's hands move down, exploring the soft bare skin of my body. There's hardly any fabric between the two of us, so that every incredible sensation can be felt.

"Make me come," I whisper against his lips, feeling safe in the boldness of telling him what I want him to do to me.

Oscar doesn't disappoint. He takes my request and

moves his hand between us. The pads of his fingertips move over the silk fabric of my panties.

"You like that?" he asks.

I can only nod my agreement. Words are getting lost in the haze of my brain. He pushes aside the fabric and presses one finger and then two into the wet folds of my pussy.

I moan in pleasure, tossing my head back as he works in and out of me.

How is it possible I'm already so close?

I've never gotten to this point so quickly with any other man before. Oscar presses down on that magic spot deep inside me, and I ride his hand faster and faster.

"Look at me," Oscar orders me in a no-nonsense tone.

Our eyes meet and lock, searing this moment between us. With only a few more pumps, I come undone in front of him. Crying out in pleasure as I hold on to him as my anchor, allowing my orgasm to wash over me but not pull me out into the undertow.

I fall forward against him, resting my head in the crook of his neck and trying to settle my breathing. With each deep breath, I try to remember everything about the scent of his skin.

The reality of what we just did begins to creep in, and I want so much to push it away. I want more of this bubble we are in. I want more of him.

"What are you thinking?" he finally asks, breaking the silence that has settled around us.

"That was—" I breathe out.

"Unexpected," he finishes.

I sit up, needing to make sure there isn't any regret in his eyes. But I'm met with a darkening look of lust from Oscar. His hands grip my hips and pulls me close against him. The feeling of his hard cock sparks another wave of pleasurable aches in my lower belly. I press my palms against his bare chest and push off him. Oscar's gaze narrows when he thinks I'm ending what we've already started, but I pull his shirt off over my head and turn for the bathroom.

"Are you coming?" I ask over my shoulder.

seven

. . .

OSCAR

Watching Mere come undone in front of me is the sexiest thing I've ever seen in my life. With the pretense of our fake relationship long gone at this point, I'm on my feet and following her into the bathroom.

The shower is already running, and I can see her nude form moving behind the cloudy glass of the door. I'm not used to feeling this untethered to my control, but that's what she does to me. From the moment we met, Mere has opened my eyes to her unique view of life. She doesn't let the binds of society dictate what she does. She lives each moment like it's her last and doesn't give a fuck what anyone thinks.

When I'm around her, I feel unburdened by the worries that tomorrow, next week, or next year will bring. I want to let loose.

I pull open the door and watch in stunned silence as the

water from the showerhead washes down every curve of her body. A body I could spend my life exploring and never get tired of.

Mere runs her hands over her head, pushing her wet hair back. "I was worried you might have changed your mind."

A mischievous grin spreads across my face, and I push down at the pajama pants around my hips, letting them fall to the floor. My cock is still raging, needing relief that only Mere can give me as it bounces against my stomach.

I step into the shower, pulling Mere against me as I lean down and kiss her with the hunger of a starving man. It's been so long since a woman has consumed me so completely that I am not sure I've ever felt this way before. I bite her bottom lip, and she opens up, allowing me to deepen the kiss.

I'm so used to being in control of every aspect of my life, but Mere takes it without even asking as she pulls back to break the kiss.

"Wha—" I start to ask but stop when I watch her lower down to her knees.

The moment her hands and lips touch the sensitive tip of my cock, my vision blurs, and I need to rest my hands against the tiled wall for support. Her tongue moves up and down the thick length, making my toes curl to keep from losing myself. The hot water starts to cool, allowing my brain to focus and formulate a plan.

I reach over and shut off the water. As sexy as this scene would be in a movie, logistically, it's a nightmare, and we don't need to slip and break something before the wedding.

"Come on," I say, urging Mere to her feet.

Leading her out of the shower, we don't go far. I want to watch her come undone again, but when I'm inside her.

"Here." I point to the counter in front of the mirror. "I'm going to watch you scream my name while I'm inside you."

The color in Mere's cheeks darkens, but the smile on her face tells me that she's more than ready for what we are about to do. I run my hand down her bare back, pushing gently until she rests her elbows on the marble sink. The soft moans of pleasure that slip out of her as I run my cock up and down the folds of her pussy, make it nearly impossible not to lose myself right here, right now.

I shift my hips forward and push inside her. She's so tight I can only move an inch at a time. It's only when I'm fully rooted inside her that I cup her breasts with each hand I lift her back up, her back to my front.

"Ready?" I growl into her ear, needing to know that she's willing to hand back the control to me.

Mere nods her head as our gazes meet in the reflection of the mirror in front of us. I move slowly at first, allowing the movement of our bodies to increase the pleasurable pressure between us. Mere rests her hands over mine as my rhythm increases.

With each pump in and out of her, the urge to feel closer to her consumes me. I wrap both arms around her and pull her against me. The sounds of pleasure coming from Mere are nearly my undoing. I need only one thing from her—to hear my name on her lips when she comes.

"Say it," I breathe, watching her inch closer to her undoing.

Mere's eyes roll back, and she screams my name as her second orgasm of the morning tears through her.

"Oscar! Oh god!"

I let myself stumble off the edge into oblivion with her into bliss. The pleasure of our shared release ripples through both of us until it slowly fades. Leaving us with only the sounds of our ragged breathing.

"That was—" I breathe out.

"Unbelievable," she finishes.

eight

. . .

MERRY

I could have easily stayed locked in our room, living off room service and orgasms, but my duties as maid of honor pulled me away. Oscar had his own best-man responsibilities to deal with as well, leaving us very little time to interact for most of the day.

There was the final dress fitting, where Katherine threw a fit because my dress was a different shade than hers and the rest of the bridesmaids. Then there was the debacle of Amy's veil getting torn and me spending a few hours driving around town trying to find anything that would work as a substitute.

"What is that?" Katherine asks, pointing to the bag in my hand from the art store in town.

"I'm going to make Amy a hair wreath," I explain. "There's no place close enough that we can get a wedding veil in time.

Tomorrow is Christmas Eve, and I don't want Amy

stressing over this so close to the wedding. And thanks to the years of making homemade Christmas decorations with my mom and my sisters, I know that I can pull something together that will work as a substitute and still be beautiful.

The other bridesmaids walk over to us and watch as I pull out all the pieces I need to assemble the headpiece. I picked out pieces of pine, fake frosted cranberries, holly berries, some fake snow spray, wire, and a hot glue gun.

"They match perfectly with all our dresses," Amy's cousin says, holding the holly berries up against the dresses hanging in the bridal suite.

"That was the plan." I smile and quickly get to work.

Everyone else works on getting the reception goodie bags prepared while talking amongst themselves. Outside the window, I can see Oscar down below helping Nathan carry in the wedding arch that was constructed for the ceremony.

"How are you doing?" I ask Amy quietly.

She's been taking all the mishaps we've been dealing with for the wedding with tremendous stride. A lesser bride would have already lost it and threatened to call off the ceremony by now.

"I'm just trying to go through my mental checklist to make sure that I'm not missing anything and leaving it to the last minute."

"Is there anything else I can do to help you?"

She leans against me and rests her head on my shoulder. "You're here. That helps more than you know."

As I continue weaving the pine and berries together into the headpiece, my mind slips back to moments of working on decorations with my mom. Pain starts to ache in my heart, and I can feel the hot sting of tears begin to burn my eyes.

"Are you okay, Mere?" Amy asks.

I nod and blink back the tears. "I think I need to take a break for a moment."

I don't want an audience for whatever is about to come next. Putting down the half-made piece, I slip quietly out of the suite. The wave of grief that was building rushes over me the moment the door clicks shut. I cover my face with my hands and slide down the wall to the floor.

Being here for Amy's wedding was a good excuse for not staying home for the holidays, but there's no saying that I wouldn't have left either way. I've never been one to deal with things head-on like my sisters. I smile or make a joke, trying to push away the feelings that come with a heavy situation—never wanting to deal with them because then I have to look ahead and face the future. In this case, a future where my mom isn't in it.

"Mere?" Oscar's voice penetrates my grief.

I try to catch my breath to speak, but the tears keep coming.

"Are you hurt?" He kneels down in front of me.

I shake my head no—not physically, at least. Oscar pulls me into his arms and sits down next to me on the floor. He doesn't speak. He just holds me until I'm able to pull myself back together.

"I'm sorry about that," I finally say, wiping at my tear-stained cheeks.

"Do you want to tell me what happened?" he asks.

My instinct to push away all that I'm feeling would be so much easier, but I surprise myself and open up to him. I tell him about my mom and what happened to her over the summer. He listens quietly as I speak.

"I'm sorry," he says when I finish. "She sounds like she was an incredible woman."

"She was the best," I agree. "I only hope I can be half the woman she was."

Oscar cups my face and tilts my head up to meet his steady gaze. "You already are. You dropped everything for a friend that needed you even when you are dealing with so much. I didn't know your mom, but I feel certain that she would be so proud of you and the woman you are."

I could never have imagined that the man in front of me, who was supposed to be my fake boyfriend for the weekend, has changed so much in such a short amount of time. The way he looks at me. The way he makes me feel safe even when I'm feeling at my lowest is beyond anything I could imagined for myself. But all at once, I remember that this between us isn't something that can last. We never promised each other anything more than this weekend, but for the first time in my life, I see the sparkle of a future.

The door of the suite opens, and Amy's head pokes out, looking around for me.

"There you are," Amy says when she sees us sitting on the floor.

I can see it in the narrowing of her eyes when she sees my puffy red eyes, her gaze swings to Oscar like he had something to do with them being there.

"It's okay," I assure her.

Amy's expression softens. "If you're sure?"

"I'm sure."

"Why don't you head into the suite and freshen up," she says to me and then points to Oscar. "I need to talk to you about some wedding stuff."

We both push to our feet, Oscar's hand linking with mine. I'm happy for the ruse, so I can push up on my toes and kiss him quickly.

"Thank you for listening," I tell him.

"Anytime."

"I'll meet you inside," Amy tells me.

I head back into the suite with one more look over my shoulder at Oscar. His gaze is still on me, sending a chill of excitement through me. I think I'm falling for him.

nine

. . .

OSCAR

"What the hell do you two think you are playing at?" Amy punches me in the arm. It doesn't hurt, but it's as startling as her outburst.

"What do you mean?"

"Oh no." She shakes her head at me. "Don't try and play dumb. Mere is my best friend, and I know everything about her life. If you two were dating for real, I would have known about it."

"It's not a big deal," I say, even though I know that's a lie. Things between us have already morphed from a fake relationship to something so much more.

"You may think you know Mere, and she puts on a great face most of the time, but she's been hurt before." Amy points at the suite door. "When the rugs been ripped out from under you too many times, you do what you can to protect yourself from getting hurt again. That's why she doesn't like to get serious with anyone. She doesn't want to imagine one future only to have it change on her."

"I won't hurt her."

"Really?" Amy puts her hands on her hips. "Does she know who you really are? Billionaire playboy with a reputation for not settling down."

The description of me stings more than I'd like to admit, even to myself. It's true that when I first found success, I went a little wild, and I haven't been able to shake that reputation since.

I can tell Amy that I've changed until I'm blue in the face, but Mere is her best friend, and she's going to do everything she can to protect her.

"I have my reasons for keeping some things to myself," I say, trying to hold back my anger.

"Merry is vulnerable right now, and I don't want her to get hurt."

"I would never hurt her."

"Not on purpose," she says. "I believe that much."

"What do you want me to say?" I ask.

"I want you to be honest with her."

My phone starts to ring, and I pull it out of my pocket. Nathan's name flashes on the screen.

"Think about what I've said." Amy reaches for the door and heads inside without another word.

The rest of the evening, I couldn't get what Amy said out of my head. I know I should tell Mere the truth about exactly who I am. I don't want any secrets between us, but Mere isn't the only one with a past.

After I finally started to settle down and grow into the man I am today, I began to look for someone more serious. And I got burned in love too. Only my heartbreak played out in tabloids, for which she sold our story to make some quick cash. It's been incredible to have someone just look at me and see the real me, not my name or what's in my bank account. But Amy's right. I need to tell her the truth. This relationship may have started out as fake, but if I hope to make it truly real, then I need to be honest with Mere.

As the countdown clock ticks closer to the wedding, I can't find a moment alone with Mere to talk for the rest of the day. She even ends up spending the night in the bridal suite making headpieces for the bridesmaids instead of in our room with me.

The following day my time is spent making multiple runs to and from the airport to pick up guests. Since it's Christmas Eve, the staff at the lodge is low, and it's all hands on deck to do our best so everything runs smoothly.

"There you are," Mere's voice says as I walk into the lodge lobby after my third trip of the day to the airport.

I have one more to make in thirty minutes before I have to race to get ready for the wedding rehearsal and the dinner afterward.

"You are a sight for sore eyes," I say leaning down and kissing her smiling face.

"I missed you," she says and then looks around to see if anyone is nearby. "I was hoping you might join me in the shower before I get ready for tonight."

My dick twitches with excitement at the memory of the last time we were in the shower together.

"I wish I could, but I have to head back out to pick up Nathan's aunt and uncle. Their flight was delayed because of the storm coming in and holiday travel." I lean close and whisper into her ear. "You have no idea how much I'd like to join you."

The soft gasp from Mere thrills me, and I want to know what other sounds I can get her to make.

"There's always tonight," she promises. "I made Amy promise no more all-nighters. We all need our beauty rest for the big day tomorrow."

At the mention of Amy, I remember that I'd planned to talk with Mere about everything. I don't have a lot of time, but I don't want to put it off.

"Every time I see that woman, she has on the greatest old lady tracksuits." Mere smiles, looking past my shoulder.

I turn, but I don't see any older woman in a tracksuit in the group of people standing around in the lobby.

"Who are you—" I start to ask when Nathan yells my name.

"My uncle just called and said their plane landed early."

Damn it.

"I'm sorry, but I've got to go." I lean down and give Mere a quick kiss before turning and heading out of the lodge.

ten

. . .

MERRY

The wedding rehearsal is the first thing about this whole weekend that has gone off without a hitch. Everyone was able to follow the instructions and understand what they needed to do for the big day tomorrow.

I hadn't planned on needing a gift for Oscar, but I thought that it wouldn't be Christmas without giving a gift for someone you care about. But when my video call with my sisters ran a bit long this afternoon, I didn't get a chance to run into town to get him anything.

Instead, I took the leftovers from the headpieces and made him an ornament. It's nothing much, but I wanted something to remember our first Christmas together.

"Is this dumb?" I ask Amy and pull out the ornament from my clutch. "I didn't have time to get Oscar anything for a gift."

Amy takes the ornament and turns it over in her hands.

"This looks just like something your mom would have made. It's not dumb at all."

"I didn't really know what to get him."

"I mean, what do you get the guy who can literally buy whatever he wants?" She laughs.

I stare at her in confusion. "What are you talking about?"

Her laughter dies almost instantly. "He didn't tell you?"

"Tell me what?"

She shakes her head, but I've known Amy most of my life. I can read her like a book, and I can see something warring inside of her.

"What was he supposed to tell me?" I ask.

"He said he would," she mumbles to herself. "It's not a big deal, Mere, but Oscar hasn't been completely honest with you."

"Honest about what?" I ask.

The familiar feeling of uneasiness in my stomach flips as I brace myself for whatever she's about to say.

"He should really be the one to tell you."

"But I'm asking you," I say, louder than I planned. A few people nearby turn to look.

"It's better if I just show you." She picks up her phone and types something in before handing it over to me.

It's an article about Oscar and why he's the most eligible bachelor in the country.

"Billionaire playboy?" I ask, looking up.

Amy shrugs. "Nathan says he's long since left those days behind him, but that's because he's worried about a woman trying to use him."

"He didn't tell me because he thinks I'm so shallow that I'd want him only for his money?"

The idea that he would think so little of me hits like a

punch to the gut. All the signs were staring me straight in the face this whole time, but I was too stupid to realize it.

When we met, he drove up in a fancy town car with a driver. And when I mentioned how Nathan's family got us a private plane to bring us here, he made a face like he didn't know what I was talking about. Then when we made plans for our fake relationship, he never told me why. He thought if I knew the truth, I'd be different around him.

I'm utterly embarrassed for not realizing any of it. He must have thought it was hilarious to play me like that.

I look around the dining hall for Oscar and see him standing and talking with some of Nathan's family. Almost as if he could feel my gaze, he glances up. The smile on his face falters as he looks between Amy and me.

"I need to go," I say, standing up and pushing my way through the other guests and out the door to the patio.

The Vermont winter wind hits me the second I walk out, but I'm too mad to care. Needing to burn off some of my fury, I pace up and down the snowy patio. I clench my fist and feel the prick of wire in the palm of my hand. I look down and see I'm still holding the ornament I made. Winding up, I toss the homemade piece out into the snow with all my strength.

"You really should be wearing a coat, dear," a voice says behind me.

I spin around and see the older woman I've been seeing in the lodge all weekend. "What are you doing out here?"

She pulls at the sides of her puffy red jacket with fake fur-lined trim. "I was getting some air until you came out."

"I'm sorry," I say. "I couldn't be in there any longer."

"Don't like weddings?"

"No." I shake my head. "I mean, yes, I like weddings,

but I just found out something about a guy I thought I knew."

Even as I say the words, I know that it was stupid of me to think that after only knowing Oscar for a few days, I should know anything about him. I'd opened up to him in more ways than I had with anyone in a long time. But he didn't think I was worthy enough to open up in the same way.

"Love, it can be a real kick in the ass sometimes," the woman says.

"Sounds to me like you don't think it's worth it, and I'm inclined to agree."

The woman smiles and shakes her head. "I wouldn't say that."

"Loving people only ever seems to hurt me. It's not worth putting myself out there. Why risk it?"

"The future is full of uncertainty. You can't predict it, and you can't run away from it. Not everyone intends to hurt the ones they love. It's human to make mistakes. And sometimes the situation is out of their control."

The way she's talking, it sounds like we aren't just talking about Oscar. My mom's face pops into my mind. But this woman couldn't know anything about that.

"It's easy to run to avoid being hurt, but sometimes those moments are what make you stronger. It's a cliché for a reason."

"My mom used to say that," I say.

She smiles. "She was a wise woman."

The cold wind kicks up again, but this time, the chill penetrates and cools my anger. I rub my hands up and down my arms to try and warm up.

"It's the season of forgiveness," she continues. "We'd

hate to see you give up on something great because of fear of yet to come."

"We?" I ask.

She only smiles and nods back towards the doors to the party. I look through the frosted glass windows and see Oscar talking with Amy. He seems upset, and now that I have a cooler head, I can see that he and I aren't so different. Our fears stem from two different reasons, but in the end, we both want the same thing—to be loved.

OSCAR

"But where did she go?" I ask Amy.

She's already chewed me out for not opening up to Mere about who I was. She only let me off the hook a bit when I explained that I couldn't tell her because of all the wedding preparations.

"She just got up and walked over there."

I turn to where she's pointing and see Mere walking back in from the patio.

"Merry!" I yell and push my way through the crowd to her. She's shivering from the cold, so I pull off my suit coat and wrap it around her. "What were you doing out there with no coat on?"

"I was just talking with—" she starts to say but stops when she looks out to the empty patio.

"We need to get you warmed up."

Mere shakes her head. "I need to tell you something."

"I need to tell you something too. Or rather, I did need to tell you something, but I guess now you know."

"I don't care about that," she says, surprising me. "I fell

in love with you before I knew the truth. I need you to know that."

I'm stunned into silence. My heart soaring at her words.

"You had your reasons for not telling me—" she says but holds up a hand to stop me from trying to interrupt and explain. "I won't lie that it hurt when I found out, but I can see why you did it. But I need you to know that the only thing I care about is you."

I've dreamed of finding someone that would love me for me, but I would have given away every penny I have to hear those words come from Merry. It's like my own Christmas wish come true.

"You aren't saying anything," she says.

I shake my head and smile from ear to ear. "I can't tell you how much I wanted to hear you say those words. I messed up not telling you, and I will make it up to you somehow."

"How about you tell me you love me too?" She chuckles.

"I love you, Merry Christmas Carol."

Mere throws her head back and laughs. "That's not my middle name."

"It's not?" I joke. "Seems like a real missed opportunity."

"I think my mom thought saddling me with a name like Merry was just festive enough."

"Well, maybe when we name our kids, we can take it to the next level."

Her eyes widen. "You see kids in our future?"

"I see limitless possibilities in our future." I wrap her tighter in my arms and lean down to press my lips against hers to warm her.

"I think we should take this up to the shower," Mere whispers against my lips.

"You read my mind."

eleven

· · ·

MERRY

"To us finally getting together this holiday," Holly holds up one of the champagne flutes that Ivy just finished pouring out.

"These are supposed to be for the ball drop," Ivy chides, but only half-heartedly.

I pick up a flute and hand it over to her before taking one for myself. "I think it's safe to say that no one expected this Christmas to turn out the way it did, but I think it turned out for the best."

We clink glasses, and each take a sip. The cold bubbles tickle my nose as I swallow the sweet liquid.

"Who knew that we'd all manage to find love?" Ivy asks. "Well, I guess someone knew."

Holly and I exchange a curious glance.

"What does that mean?" I ask.

"You guys are going to think I'm crazy, but I kept

having these crazy dreams about this older woman who kept pushing me toward Luke."

We all turn and glance out the kitchen door into the living room, where Ivy's Luke is laughing with Oscar and Holly's Jonas.

"That's weird," Holly says, taking another sip of champagne. "I met an older woman outside my work who did the same with Jonas and me."

The hairs on the back of my neck stand up as I think about the woman at the lodge with all the crazy tracksuits. Despite my claims of talking with her multiple times and one last time on the lodge patio, Oscar has no memory of seeing her.

"Did she have short, silvery white hair?" I ask.

"Yes," both Ivy and Holly say at the same time.

The three of us exchange a look of disbelief, each thinking the same thing, but no one wants to say the words out loud.

"She was at the lodge—" I start to explain but stop when Oscar pops his head into the door.

"The countdown to midnight is about to start," he says.

Ivy and Holly each grab a flute for their guys and walk out. I'm not sure we can believe that the same person visited each of us before Christmas.

"You okay?" Oscar asks.

I pick up the last flute and hand it to him. "Yeah, all good."

"Okay, because I've been looking forward to kissing you all night to thank you for my gift." He wraps his arm around my waist and pulls me close.

"What gift?" I ask.

Oscar's head tilts in confusion. "The one you left on the

bedside table this morning for me. There was a note and everything."

"I don't—" I start to say, but when Oscar holds up the ornament that I made him and threw into the snow on Christmas Eve, the words dry up on my lips.

"Ten, nine, eight," everyone in the living room starts to chant.

"Come on, you guys!" Holly yells out.

Oscar takes my hand and leads us out of the kitchen and into the living room for the final three seconds.

"Happy New Year!" Everyone cheers and clinks their glasses with one another.

I turn to Oscar as he leans in to kiss me. "Happy New Year."

"It's going to be the best year," I tell him.

"What do we have planned?"

I smile, loving that for the first time in my life, I am able to plan beyond the next few days ahead of me. "The rest of our lives."

epilogue

. . .

A few years later...

OSCAR

I peek into our daughter's room and see her sleeping on Merry's chest as she rocks her in the rocking chair.

"Is she asleep?" I ask.

Mere shakes her head as Noelle makes soft little sounds like she's trying to fight sleep, but it's quickly winning out.

So much has changed in the last few years since our first Christmas together, and until Noelle was born, it was my favorite Christmas. Now I have both my Christmas girls, and I couldn't be happier.

Noelle makes a little humming sigh, and that is our confirmation that she's finally given into sleep.

"She's going to be impossible to get to sleep when she's older, and she has to wait for Santa," Mere whispers.

I smile, knowing she's right, yet I still can't wait to see her little face light up on Christmas morning when she sees presents under the tree.

"I can't wait," I whisper back.

"Me too."

Mere stands up and lays Noelle gently into her crib. We stand there quietly, looking down at her peaceful little face as she dreams. I wrap my arms around Mere and pull her against me. I couldn't have dreamed I'd ever get to be this happy. I thought I was content with a life without love before Mere, but now I have more than any man should be lucky enough to have.

"Merry Christmas," I say and lean in to kiss Mere's neck.

She sighs and tilts her head to give me more access. "I know the plan after putting her down was to wrap presents, but I have something else in mind."

"Shower?" I ask, kissing a trail up to her ear.

"I was going to say bubble bath, but either way gets me wet."

"Not in front of the baby," I feign shock and turn a smiling Merry in my arms. But before she can say anything, I lean down and lift her up and onto my shoulder. She chuckles quietly as I walk us both out of our daughter's room.

"Wait," she says, and I set her down.

She jumps up and wraps her legs around my waist as I grab her ass to hold onto her. "That's better."

"I love you." I chuckle.

"Now and forever."

✳

Read more from Lana Dash!
Follow her on Facebook.

about the authors

Kali Hart writes short & sweet with plenty of heat. Instalove is the name of her game. She loves penning protective heroes with hearts of gold who'll do anything for the women they love. As a military veteran herself who served in the Army and completed a tour overseas in Iraq, Kali often writes characters with military experience and backgrounds. Because who doesn't love a good man—and sometimes woman—in uniform?

Kate Tilney is the author of more than 130 steamy romances. A Midwest girl whose heart is in the mountains, her stories star curvy heroines finding true love and a happily ever after, usually with a mountain man or fire-fighter. When she isn't looking up pictures of bearded men in flannel shirts (all for research, of course), Kate can be found making TikToks or curling up with one of her cats in front of a fake fireplace, pretending she's in a cabin.

Lana Dash writes short and steamy romances filled with heart, humor, and happily ever afters that will leave you swiping for more. From blue-collar bad boys to rugged mountain men, you will find a book boyfriend to swoon over in the span of your hour-long lunch break.

Milton Keynes UK
Ingram Content Group UK Ltd.
UKHW031020011224
451693UK00004B/586

9 798224 321995